W9-CZX-351

nice girls ENDURE

BY CHRIS STRUYK-BONN

Switch Press
a capstone imprint

Nice Girls Endure
is published by Switch Press
A Capstone Imprint
1710 Roe Crest Drive
North Mankato, Minnesota 56003
www.mycapstone.com

Copyright © 2016 Chris Struyk-Bonn

All rights reserved.

No part of this publication may be reproduced in whole or in part, or stored in a retrieval system, or transmitted in any form or by any means, electronic, mechanical, photocopying, recording, or otherwise, without written permission of the publisher.

Library of Congress Cataloging-in-Publication Data

Name: Struyk-Bonn, Christina, author.

Title: Nice girls endure / by Chris Struyk-Bonn.

Description: North Mankato, Minnesota : Switch Press, a Capstone imprint, [2016] | Summary: Sixteen-year-old Chelsea has always been overweight, and now in high school she is being unmercifully teased by other students, and even her mother gives her no support, despite her beautiful singing voice—but in film class she is assigned work on a film with Melody and for the first time she finds someone other than her father who does not criticize her, and finally finds the confidence to try out for the school choir.

Identifiers: LCCN 2016014789| ISBN 9781630790479 (jacketed hardcover) | ISBN 9781630790462 (ebook pdf)

Subjects: LCSH: Obesity—Juvenile fiction. | Bullying—Juvenile fiction.| Motion pictures—Juvenile fiction. | Singing—Juvenile fiction. |Fathers and daughters—Juvenile fiction. | Mothers and daughters—Juvenile fiction. | Self-confidence—Juvenile fiction. | High schools—Juvenile fiction. | Friendship—Juvenile fiction. | CYAC: Obesity—Fiction. | Bullying—Fiction. | Motion pictures—Fiction. | Singing—Fiction. | Fathers and daughters—Fiction. | Mothers and daughters—Fiction.| Self-confidence—Fiction.| High schools—Fiction. | Schools—Fiction. |Friendship—Fiction.

Classification: LCC PZ7.S92772 Ni 2016 | DDC 813.6 [Fic]—dc23

LC record available at https://lccn.loc.gov/2016014789

Cover image credits: Shutterstock: chronicler, makar, P. Chinnapong

Book design: Kay Fraser

Printed and bound in China.
009578F16

To my family

One

My parents tell me all the time that I should enjoy my teenage years, that these should be the happiest, most carefree days of my life, that this is the time for me to become independent and figure out who I truly am. You know what I say to that? What a bunch of crap.

My happiest memory goes back to when I was four years old. Yes, four years old. That's twelve years ago, and I swear I haven't been happy and carefree since.

We were at the city pool, I think, although my recollection could be slightly off. Memory can do that.

Mom was there in my memory, but she wouldn't get in the water. Instead she lay in the sun, her hair perfectly rolled and perfectly dry.

But Dad was in the water with me, and that's where I'm confused by my memory. He doesn't swim now, but in that moment, we splashed and shrieked, bobbed and paddled, spit water from our mouths, and floated on our backs. And then Dad picked me up and threw me into the air. I'll always remember that, looking up, not down, and feeling like I'd become part of the open sky — the clouds like wisps around me, the ground far enough away to not matter, and the feeling of weightlessness

5

wafting around me through the touch of a breeze on my wet skin.

And then I came down, and Dad caught me. He threw me up again, but Mom rushed to the edge of the pool, yelling at him to stop.

So he did.

But he whispered to me, "Always look up, Chelsea. Hold your head high."

I can't do it. Since that day at the pool, that sensation of weightlessness has eluded me, and I've been looking at the ground instead of the sky. I've been looking at the gray, cold concrete, and I've been looking at feet. My feet. And that part, at least, is something okay, because my feet are the best physical attribute I have. My toes are long and narrow, with just enough flesh covering the bony parts. My toenails are strong and nicely rounded. I paint them at least once a week — more if I need to. I own thirty-seven pairs of shoes — almost all of them backless with open toes. I want the world to see my beautiful feet.

Most people don't notice feet. They don't care that mine are perfect, pretty, because they see other things about me that they don't like, and that's how they judge me. My dad says, "People should look up and down. They should notice everything, even little details, not just the first impression. If other people can't see you for who you really are, then you don't need them."

But he's wrong. I do need them. Dad doesn't understand this. He doesn't have friends — my parents don't play cards with the neighbors or go on cycling expeditions through Spain with their old college buddies. When we invite people over, we invite his parents, or my mom's dad, Grandpa Reece.

"Who needs friends when you have family?" my dad says.

I guess I've adopted his philosophy. I don't have friends either.

Two

School is the worst part of my life, and I spend more time there than anywhere else, unless you count sleep. I hate school. The idiots who invented high school sure got it wrong. They decided that throwing people together who are as different as primary colors was a good idea. They decided that they should take the druggies, the jocks, the brainiacs, the socially inept — we all have labels — throw them together in a little box, shake up the box, and tell them to get along. When they inevitably don't all get along, the kids are thrown out of the box as "punishment."

If I could get thrown out, I'd be thrilled. I'd go home, open up a shoe store called Chelsea's, and never look back. Not once.

But nice girls don't get thrown out of school. We just endure, which is what I'm doing right now. Accounting sucks. I know that if I open my own shoe store I'll probably need to know something about accounting, so it isn't the class itself that makes sweat drip down my back.

It's Nicholas Dunn.

Nicholas Dunn thinks he's the only guy on the planet who looks good. He struts his stuff every chance he gets by striding back and forth at the front of the room and flirting with the teacher, Ms. Sandell. Of course Ms. Sandell devours every word Nicholas Dunn says and thinks he's absolutely adorable. I've even seen her check out his butt before. And every time he gets out of his seat, every girl in the room looks up. He wears tight T-shirts that show off his abdominal muscles and well-developed pectorals.

He's beautiful in an asshole sort of way.

"Hey, chubs. You do your assignment? Can I take a look at it? I'm talking to you. You-hoo, jelly-belly.

What's your name, anyway? Hey, anyone know what her name is?"

I'm fully aware that he's talking to me, but until he can communicate in a civilized manner, I'm not answering.

"Chelsea. Is that your name? Chelsea? Did you do the assignment?"

I glance up at Nicholas Dunn, my eyes wide.

"I'm sorry, what did you say?" I ask.

"Chubby Chelsea. That's got a nice ring to it. You like to dance, Chelsea? You like to shake your bootie?"

I give him a tight smile, squint, and look back down at my desk.

Yeah, I do my homework, but he'll never get anywhere near it. I wish we didn't have assigned seats in this class. I wish I sat halfway across the room from Nicholas Dunn. I wish I knew how to put him in his place, give him back worse than he gives me, but I just don't think that way. At night, while I'm lying in bed, I think of all kinds of witty replies, like, "My, what a wide vocabulary you have, Mr. Dunn." Or I'd say something that really puts him in his place like, "Squeeze your bod into a Speedo, Nicholas, and I'm sure Ms. Sandell will gladly give you an A."

Okay, so I'm not the type to come up with witty

one-liners, even when lying in bed at night, but I do know that I hate Nicholas Dunn. I hate him like the mouse hates the cat — in a terrified sort of way.

Three

Nicholas Dunn doesn't know anything about me. I sing way more than I dance. I see every musical I can find and watch them fifty times over until I know every word of every song, and so does my dad, who sings better than Fred Astaire. We've watched *My Fair Lady* so often, our British accents are perfect. We have a DVD player in our partially finished basement, so we blast the sound and I sing along with Audrey Hepburn through every song. My favorite scene is the one at the horse races where she screams, "Move your bloomin' arse!" in front of all the high-class people.

When she's dancing at the ball, I even dance with her.

Unless Mom is home. If Mom is home, I don't dance. Sometimes, when Mom doesn't have desperate taxpayers lined up outside her office door, she comes home early. If she comes home early, my song and dance session is over.

"I'm so glad to see you exercising," she says, standing halfway down the stairs to the basement and smiling at me like we're all on some reality TV show and have to grin for the camera. Her tan slacks and cream blouse make her look like a vanilla ice-cream cone. "Keep it up, Chelsea. That's great."

I don't need her to say that. I don't want her to say that. My mom is not overweight. She has never been overweight in her life — oh, she tells me that she needs to drop ten pounds here, a couple of inches there, a nip, a tuck. She still fits into clothes from twenty years ago, from before she had me. She has no idea what it's like to hate going to the mall because the clothes are either too tight or shapeless, or to look at yourself in the mirror and know that losing fifty pounds wouldn't be unreasonable. She believes that if I exercise, the weight will drop off. The pounds will fall to the floor like molted feathers. She'll be able to sweep up the excess that was her daughter, and put it out in the trash.

Sorry, Mom. It doesn't work that way. Not with me.

Not with my dad, either. I inherited everything I am from my father: his dark brown curly hair, his round face, his dimples, his weight. I am a female clone of my father, except that he's six inches taller than I am and a hundred pounds heavier.

We don't really talk about it.

Four

My favorite class is film as literature.

I walked into class on the first day of school and almost turned around and walked right back out again. Marcus Vemen, a kid I went to school with since kindergarten, was sitting in the front row, and knowing Marcus's less-than-stellar skills in English, he was taking this class for an easy English credit.

But then I sat down in one of the tiniest desks ever, probably inherited from Frazier Elementary School, which had been shut down, and Mr. Butler turned on a movie that very first day. It was *Cool Hand Luke*. Now I'm not saying that *Cool Hand Luke* is the best movie ever made, and that everyone should run out and purchase a copy, but it sucked me right in. I wanted Paul Newman to pierce my soul with those sky-blue eyes. And then we watched *The African Queen*, *Casablanca*, and *North by Northwest* — movies I'd never even heard about until this class. They were old — a couple were even black-and-white old — but crisp and clean and loaded with substance. I loved them all. No one swears in those movies. The women never get called *lard ass*, *wide load*, or *tubby*. They were gentlemen back then. They had depth. Now guys just talk about parkour and smoking pot and how girls need to show more skin. They don't open car doors for girls; they don't throw their jackets over mud puddles. Humphrey Bogart, Paul Newman, Cary Grant — now they were decent. They didn't swear, they didn't burp, they didn't call women names in public. That's what guys should really be like.

That first day of school, I fell in love with film as literature I. But then it was the end of the period. Mr. Butler handed out the syllabus, and I packed up my stuff and I was ready to leave. That old black-and-white movie had made me completely forget that I was wedged into the miniscule desk like a big cat in a shoe box. I tried to squeeze my way out, slide my stomach and hips past the opening intended for six-year-olds, but my pocket hooked on the bottom of the seat and the whole thing tipped over when I stood up. Two guys and a girl had stopped to watch me extricate myself and all three of them were grinning. I knew what their lunch topic would be for the day. I squashed my books against my boobs, trying to hide them, but there's no hiding double D, and slinked past them out the door.

Mr. Butler asked me, the next time I showed up for class, if I would like to sit at the table in the back of the room. My face turned pink and a rash of prickly red bumps swept up both arms. I know he was trying to be nice, but it was embarrassing. I just wanted to watch the movies without anyone noticing me, even Mr. Butler.

"No thank you," I said, a small smile on my face. "I'm fine."

Mr. Butler is still my favorite teacher.

Five

I love my dad. I love him every second of the day with all my heart. Our favorite pastime is to watch old musicals and sing along. We've seen *Oliver Twist*, *Fiddler on the Roof*, and *Oklahoma!* approximately a hundred times each. If it isn't football season, we watch movies every night. Dad will make some of his double chocolate brownies with mocha frosting or his macadamia nut caramel popcorn, and we'll watch the whole movie through, singing the songs with the characters and laughing at all of the funny scenes.

My dad thinks I'm beautiful. He truly does. He tells me all the time how lovely I am, what a beautiful daughter he has, how he couldn't have asked for anyone even remotely better than me.

I smile and feel beautiful around my father. It's the

best part of my day — the only time when I can smile and be myself without holding back or pulling in my shoulders.

For my dad, I do well in school and stick it out. I can't disappoint him. He's already set up a fund for me, a shoe-store fund. Dad says that after I get my degree in business, after I finish school, he'll invest in the startup of the store and he knows his investment will pay off in the end. My dad believes in me. He says he's betting on a sure thing.

Six

The neighbor girls, on the other hand, do not love me, and I do not love them. We moved into this neighborhood, Happy Valley, two years ago, when the houses were just going up and the paint still smelled like a new start. Our house has a two-car garage, two-and-a-half bathrooms, and a kitchen with stainless-steel appliances. The house we lived in when I was born was one hundred years old and everything in it fell apart at the touch: the tile in the shower crumbled randomly, the faucets rattled in their sockets, the stairs creaked, the floors sloped, and paint curled and flaked from the ceilings.

When we moved into the new house, everything worked. The bathroom door didn't need to be pulled up at an angle to avoid scraping on the floor. The cupboards in the kitchen didn't fall open at random times. The carpeting in the bedroom felt so good on my feet, I knew it had to be extra plush with a little angora.

And then the new neighbors bought the house next door. The girls, all under eight years old and usually wearing matching pink dresses, white tights, and buckled black shoes, didn't look real. They looked like porcelain dolls with their pursed lips, dimpled cheeks, and blue eyes framed by dark lashes.

When they first moved in, I watched them in fascination.

For about two days.

Three days after they moved in, I walked out the door on my way to school and all three girls stood in a row on their front doorstep. I was running late that day and slammed the door to the house behind me. I turned around to find three replicated Barbies peering up at me with their baby-blue eyes, their hair in pigtails and ribbons. The oldest opened her mouth and chanted.

"Fatty, fatty, two-by-four. Couldn't fit through the bathroom door. So she did it on the floor. Fatty, fatty, two-by-four."

The other two girls picked it up, and all three of them chanted at me from behind perfect round faces and little dimpled cheeks. Their mother came out of the house and laughed, like the girls were being oh-so cute, and they climbed into their Subaru Outback, the youngest one still standing at the curb chanting. She didn't even have her eyes open, didn't even break between the words, but chanted one long string of mean that meant nothing to her, but everything to me.

The rhyme followed me to school and all day long I sang the song to myself. I couldn't help it, but I wished my plastic-doll neighbors had been singing "Somewhere Over the Rainbow."

Seven

I dread yearly physicals almost as much as I fear school and avoid the creepy neighbor girls. My mom insists on coming with me, and even though she doesn't come into the examination room anymore, she still sits in the waiting area. When I'm done seeing the doctor, they have a mini conference about me.

This year the doctor decides that I should be present

for the mini conference with my mother.

"Chelsea really is a girl with unique endowments," says Dr. Lawrence while patting me on the shoulder. "I see no health issues currently, such as shortness of breath, asthma, heart disease, diabetes, or any of the other health problems that often do accompany being overweight, but she could develop these issues if she doesn't take care of herself and lose the extra pounds. I understand that you've tried various diet programs?"

Mom and Dr. Lawrence look at me with patronizing smiles and each of them claims an arm to pat.

"We've tried a couple," says Mom, "but I always worry about how young she is. She's only sixteen. Isn't it dangerous to diet when still a child?"

"Oh, I'm not talking about anything severe," the doctor says. "I'm talking about eating healthfully, exercising regularly, and shedding the weight. Chelsea could easily stand to lose thirty pounds. At five-foot-six and one hundred and seventy pounds, her BMI is twenty-seven point five percent. That puts her well into the overweight category."

Mom pats my arm. "Do you know what BMI is, honey? Dr. Lawrence, could you explain that to her?"

"It's a height-to-weight ratio. If Chelsea grows six inches in the next two years and gains no weight, she'll no longer be overweight." Doctor Lawrence chuckles when she says this and pats my other arm, as if this is such a great joke.

I haven't grown since I was fourteen — grown taller, that is.

"What diet program would you suggest?" Mom asks.

I'm sitting on the examination table studying my toes as I swing them back and forth. This morning I painted my toenails blue with tiny white stars. It's a nice color against the olive tone of my feet. I can tell that I'll need a shower when I get home — I feel sticky, sweaty, nauseated. I hate feeling sticky, feeling like I might smell, so I shower a lot. I'm very clean.

"Calorie Counters," says Dr. Lawrence, and hands my mom a card.

"Chelsea," says Dr. Lawrence, taking my hand and peering at me. I look at her. While I am sitting on the examination table, we're almost the same height. I don't like her. I've never liked her, and she's been my doctor since before I was born. She's thin, athletic, runs two marathons a year, and has no idea what I like to do or what I'm good at. She's never even noticed my perfect feet.

"You need to do this for yourself," she says. My hand is sandwiched between both of hers. My dad is probably home right now choosing a movie for tonight and popping some popcorn. "No one can make you lose the weight. You have to want to do it. You have to care about yourself and your own health."

I nod. I know this is expected of me so I bob my head and smile.

"And boys. All those cute boys in high school. Don't you want to go on dates with them?" Mom says and winks at me. "Isn't there some special guy you'd like to please?"

"And let me in on your secret sometime. You have such gorgeous curls in that pretty hair of yours," Dr. Lawrence says.

I get a good grip on my smile so it doesn't slip. I always give Dr. Lawrence the patented Chelsea smile — mouth tipped up at the corners, eyes slightly narrowed, dimples showing. If she doesn't care to get to know me, I'm not going to let her see the real me. If my dad had said something about my gorgeous hair, I would have believed him, but not Dr. Lawrence. Not my mom.

I shuffle out of the doctor's office with Mom, who is already on her cell phone, making an appointment for me with Calorie Counters. My humiliation will soon be publicized even more than it already is.

I know there's nothing wrong with me. I know that I'm healthy. I don't even eat all that badly. I have fruits and vegetables every day; I eat whole grains and small portions of meat. So why does every snack I eat attach to my hips, stick to my butt, thicken my arms? I see people at school loading their trays with fries, burgers, shakes, and onion rings, but they aren't overweight. They don't seem to have to worry. Why?

According to the doctor and my mom, much of this has to do with heredity. They say it's all from my dad's side, as if it's somehow his fault. But you know what? I wouldn't give my dad up for anyone in the world. He loves me. Me. He doesn't care about the weight.

Eight

Sometimes at school I'm invisible. Other students don't know how to look at me so they just avoid it altogether. In sociology, we are supposed to examine our family history collaboratively. Individually, we bring in family trees with pictures on them and we're assigned to share these in a group — examine traits that we've inherited, both personality traits and physical traits.

When we're supposed to get into groups, I head to the bathroom. I take my time, fluff my hair, straighten my clothes, adjust the straps on my shoes. When I come back to class, the groups are already established, so I sit in the corner and examine my family tree by myself.

No one approaches me. No one asks for me to join their group. The teacher doesn't even notice.

I turn in my family tree without the discussion. Mrs. Temple's comment is, "Well, Chelsea, I can certainly see where you got your dimples."

Nine

Our first Calorie Counters meeting is Tuesday night. Mom is chirpy and bubbly, jumping around the house like we're going to the circus. I'm about as excited as a dead horse. I feel almost sick at the thought of hanging out in a room full of overweight people, all talking about their triumphs and failures: how they lost ten pounds in two weeks, and wasn't that amazing, but they gained it all back with a few more pounds because they were sick the following week and ate too much soup and ice cream. I feel physically ill, like I'm coming down with the flu and am worried that my hardened exterior won't hold up under scrutiny. It's one thing when some skinny kid calls you *wide load*, but it's something else when another overweight person puts her arm around your shoulders and says, "I understand, dear. We all understand."

What the hell do they understand? Nothing. They know nothing about me. They don't know that I like to sing in the shower, that I can sing really well. They don't know that my feet are way better than Adele's, who would never dare put her feet on one of her album covers, and that I know more about musicals than anyone else on the planet. Will they care that I don't want to be there? Will they understand that? Of course not. They'll just think I should be there and that I'm making a wise choice.

By the time we get to the strip mall, navigate between a closed post office and a Hallmark store with no one in it, and locate the Calorie Counters storefront, which looks like a nudie bar with no windows and no lights, I've broken out in a rash. I've got flaming red skin up my chest and neck, and even have patches of it on my face. I try not to scratch. That just makes it worse, but not scratching means I don't know what to do with my shaking hands, so I scratch and squirm. Being nervous and scared is uncomfortable in so many ways.

"This will be fine," says my mom, patting me on the arm.

"I might be contagious," I say, pulling the collar of my sweater down and showing her the rash.

"Oh, honey, you're just a little flushed. I get excited too when I try something new."

Mom beams at me.

Sometimes I wonder if she's really my mom. Maybe my real mom disappeared years ago, ran out on me when she noticed I was overweight in kindergarten and never looked back. Maybe this is some fake mom — some robot mom who is programmed to act excited and bubbly when it is obvious that her daughter is terrified of going into the Calorie Counters clinic. She even looks a bit robotic, with her light brown hair styled into fake round curls that still hold the shape of the roller. Her face is long and horsey, not round like mine; her green eyes lost out to Dad's brown ones when I was born; and her eyelashes are pale, not black. For this exciting outing, she has applied foundation, blush, lipstick, and a touch of green eye shadow that went out of fashion sometime in the late eighties.

I cannot believe she is doing this to me.

The clinic is way too bright — like a hospital, and the head person greets us like she's the prom queen.

"You must be Chelsea," she says and shakes my hand. "I'm Bridgette."

She does look me in the eyes. I'll give her that.

"Why don't you come with me and we'll get started."

She leads me into a private room, and Mom tromps in too.

"Mrs. Duvay, I'm afraid this is a private consultation. You will have to wait outside."

And that's when I start to like Bridgette.

For a minute, Mom looks like she's about to argue. She looks like she might blurt something out, like, "But she's only sixteen and can't possibly find success in life on her own. I must help her." But she holds her tongue, purses her lips into a fake smile, and turns around.

Bridgette leads me into a cute little room completely decorated and painted with pastels. The chairs are light blue, the walls are light green, and the scale is light pink. I wonder how many men have been weighed on that scale. The overhead fluorescent light makes Bridgette look a bit ill.

"Have a seat, Chelsea," she says.

She sits in the other seat and leans back. She looks me right in the face — no fear, no avoidance, and waits until the silence in the room becomes awkward.

"Chelsea, do you want to be here?" she asks.

I find myself blinking about eight hundred times. She's a mind reader; she's psychic; she's freaking me out.

I don't say anything.

"I'll tell you right now, Chelsea, this won't work if you don't want to be here. Walk out that door right now, honey, and I'll tell your mom that you're too young, that you're not in the right mental place, whatever. I'll make up an excuse, but don't be here if you don't want to be."

I position my mouth into the small, tolerant smile that I've developed for all idiots. I open my mouth to say something, but I have no words. I only show my dimples and shut my mouth again.

Now that we're alone together, her prom queen routine is gone. Bridgette is earnest, all business. She's tall and big-boned, with a wide face and high cheekbones. Her plaid skirt and dark green sweater make her look like a model for women in positions of power. I like her. She's real.

"Do you want to be here, Chelsea?" she asks again.

I know what she wants me to say. She wants me to say no, I don't want to be here. She can tell that dread is flashing across my skin in the form of a red rash, but at the same time, I have my mom and Dr. Lawrence to answer to. They want me here. They believe I should want this. They want me to do this for myself.

"Uh, yeah," I finally say. "I want to be here. My health may eventually be at risk. My BMI is too high, and I could eventually get diabetes or heart disease or meningococcal disease." I don't really believe that, but I know how to tell people what they want to hear.

She looks at me for a long time. She searches my

face, glances at my hands, waits for me to change my mind.

I give her my practiced smile again, and she finally nods.

"All right," she says. "Let's get you weighed."

Calorie Counters Meeting #1

Weight Loss Goal: 28 pounds

Ten

On the first day of second semester of my sophomore year, February first, it snows. Cold flakes drop from the sky in a curtain of white, and the accumulation starts with light patches and then deeper drifts. We hardly ever get snow in Oregon — ice rain maybe, flakes that masquerade as snow but are really white raindrops that disappear when they hit the ground. But five weeks into the year, we get honest-to-goodness cold snow, and school is canceled.

I watch from the window as the white flakes float to the ground and accumulate and don't melt away. Before nine o'clock in the morning, three inches layer onto the lawns and streets, causing traffic to stop. The neighbor's SUV remains in the driveway, and the three little girls in matching red snowsuits run out into their front yard. They attempt to roll snowballs, but the dusting of snow doesn't clump, and their sad little snowman is merely a mound with a carrot jutting out of it.

Mom goes to work even though the roads are bad and she probably doesn't have to, and Dad's job as a crane operator on major construction projects means he always leaves for work early. I will have the entire day to myself.

Outside the girls kick through their snow mound and then flop down on the ground, waving their arms and legs to make snow angels. But their true selves are revealed, and the trampled impressions look more like devils than angels.

I put on my coat, pull on a stocking cap, mittens, boots, and glide out the back door, quietly shutting it behind me so the girls won't hear. I look at the perfect expanse in the backyard — the bushes with caps, the trees with frosting — and I carefully lie down in the middle of the yard. My arms know what to do and they smooth the snow into mounds at the top and bottom of their arch. The snowflakes melt onto my face like wet kitten noses. I squint my eyes to watch them fall in pinprick showers.

The backyard is quiet, peaceful, and I rest in the snow for a long time, welcoming its dampness as it seeps into my clothes. The world feels clean, freshly coated in white paint, doused by a heavy layer of something that feels honest and likeable — something that forgives. Nothing to worry about here. No one to fear.

I sit up, brace myself on my arms, and stand, being careful not to ruin my angel. I turn to look, and it's perfect. I wish it would stay forever, but I know that by tomorrow my angel self will be gone, having melted or blown away, and my true self will still suffer from imperfections that no one, sometimes not even myself, can get beyond.

Eleven

Over the course of film as literature I, Mr. Butler had redeemed himself in my eyes. He didn't invite me to sit at the table in the back of the room again, but gave me A's on all my papers, and allowed us to watch *It's a Wonderful Life* at Christmastime. Second semester, when I start taking film as literature II, I begin to question his judgment once more.

On the first day of the class he hands out a paper with a one-word title in bold at its top: *Autobiography*. Right away I get a queasy sensation in my stomach.

"This semester you will not only observe films, you will create one of your own," Mr. Butler explains. "This film you create will be due in May, on premiere day, and you will show it to the class. The film will showcase you. Who are you? What is your personality? What are your interests? Talents? Pet peeves? You must capture all of that in a five- to ten-minute film."

My hands shake. I've loved this class so much and now Mr. Butler is removing my anonymity and forcing me to expose myself. I don't know if he'll be able to maintain favorite-teacher status in my eyes. I don't mean to, but I let out this huge sigh and the girl beside me turns to look at me. I pretend I don't notice.

We've been sitting together in the back of the room all year. She talks incessantly but doesn't seem to expect an answer, so our relationship consists of passing papers back and forth or borrowing an occasional pencil. She's usually wearing something bizarre, like a square-dancing outfit or a cowboy hat.

She raises her hand.

"Mr. Butler," she says, "would we actually have to appear in the film?"

Mr. Butler chews on the cap to his pen and furrows his brow.

"Interesting question, Melody." Mr. Butler scratches the bald patch at the top of his head and combs through his mustache with his fingers. "You wouldn't have to appear in the film if you could show who you are by other means."

I realize I'm holding my breath.

She nods.

And then I dare to turn my head and acknowledge the presence of this person who clearly understands that I don't want to have anything to do with filming myself for the autobiography. She wears a flower-child dress — long and willowy in deep green. Her blond hair hangs down her back. She has tied a bandana over her head — a bright red one that matches the stockings I can see just below her ankle-length skirt. Her shoes have holes everywhere — they were once flat blue sneakers with white stripes.

Sometimes she looks punk: leopard skin tights and black leather, topped with pink hair. Today she looks like a hippie. I haven't been able to categorize her yet. Chameleon? Drama geek? Confused?

"Chelsea, right?" she says to me.

I give her my little safe smile. Smile and nod. Keep everyone happy. Pretend that you don't mind their

31

attention and aren't breaking out in a sweat because you're worried they'll criticize you and say something cruel and critical.

"You have the most beautiful feet I've ever seen," she says.

I glance down at my backless shoes with the open toes and for the first time in a long time, my forced little smile gets bigger and becomes real.

Twelve

Dad played football in high school and college, but in junior high he'd been told not to play because he was an angry, aggressive kid, and he'd been taking out his frustrations on the other players. He got over that with years of counseling and became a skilled player.

Because of his height and weight, he played defensive end. He still watches football every chance he gets, and because he's watched it ever since I was a kid, I know more about football than a lot of guys do. I know the positions, I know the best players, and I can often tell when and why a play doesn't work. I've listened to Nicholas Dunn criticize our school's team, and he doesn't know what he's talking about.

But whenever I watch football, I get frustrated. I mean, here's a sport that pays millions of dollars to overweight men for being overweight. There's a limit to how overweight they can be, but still. These huge guys are hired because they are huge, athletic guys, and use their weight to their advantage. They smash other players flat. They ambush them. They pulverize the other team. When the really big guys take out the quarterback, everyone groans because the QB might not get up again.

Just like sumo wrestling. These guys are paid to be huge; they are supposed to be gargantuan — the more rotund, the more respected.

Where is there an occupation for overweight women? Where is it okay for large women to be really good at, well, being large? The place where women might gain an iota of benefit for being large is in comedy. Or maybe in movies. What kind of choices are those? Large women are good for one thing, apparently: making people laugh. No respect is given to them at all. When men throw their weight around, people cheer. Equality of the sexes has not reached all corners.

Thirteen

When we return from our visit to Calorie Counters, Mom asks Dad if he would like to join our weight-loss project.

"We can do our calorie counting together," she says. "We'll make it a family project."

Dad laughs his belly-shaking, earth-thumping laugh, his dark brown beard bobbing while his cheeks and his nose turn red.

"Cynthia, you will not lay a hand on my dietary needs. You will not meddle in my choice of foods," he says. "I understand your need to categorize, organize, and arrange, and I certainly understand that all of this stems from your horrible family history, but I don't see the need to count my calories, and you will not do it for me."

Mom looks down at her feet. By choice, she has organized her sisters out of her life, and her father has only a peripheral allocation of her time. Her mother was a drunk who slapped and berated the girls. Because my grandmother was so unpredictable, my mother has chosen to become disciplined and structured. There are no junk drawers in our house. Everything has its place. The hall closet, which we call the linen closet but contains no linens, is lined with plastic organizers and jars. We have jars for paper clips, screws, thumbtacks, and loose keys. We have bins for miscellaneous manuals, bank statements, coupons, and maybe-we'll-want-them-someday flyers. I challenge anyone to find a piece of paper lying around in our house.

My dad's talents lie in operating large cranes and in getting to the core of my mother. It's pretty obvious that my dad understands psychology. He majored in it in college, but he never finished his degree. He claims, though, that he'd rather operate a crane than work on people's psychological problems. He thinks that some psychologists do more damage than good. I think that if Dad had chosen to become a psychologist, he'd be brilliant. He'd be loving, nonjudgmental, and kind. He'd be a great listener.

In the meantime I guess he can operate a crane and analyze my mother on the side.

"Did you ask Chelsea if she wanted to join Calorie Counters?" he asks. "Did you give her the choice to say no?"

My mom barely lifts her head but glances at me quickly.

Mom didn't ask me — I had no choice — and now she has decided that she can be in charge of my life.

She arranges our meals according to the Calorie Count Plan and in this plan I am allowed fifteen hundred calories a day, which are represented by fifteen stickers, one hundred calories each. She posts a chart on the fridge with all our food allotments organized into nice accountant-like grids and printed on paper with little celery stalks or other vegetables in the upper right-hand corner. Every week I get one hundred extra calories that I may choose to consume in any way I like, represented by a pile of smiling brussels sprouts. Once I've reached the end of my fifteen hundred calories, or fifteen vegetable stickers on my chart, no more food that day.

I feel like I'm locked in a house with a crazed dietician. Mom has the whole calorie system memorized already, and anytime I even look at food, she tells me how many stickers that certain item is worth.

"Oh, Chelsea," she'll say. "Are you sure you want to eat that bagel? That's three of your fifteen stickers right there. Then you'll only have twelve more stickers for the entire day."

Like I can't do the math myself.

"Oh, Chelsea," she'll say, jumping out from behind the fridge door as soon as I open it. "Cheese is full of fat. You'll lose a sticker just by having a slice or two."

I'm pretty sure she's doing some generous rounding up. She's got me so paranoid about what I'm looking at that I've decided not to eat anything. I'll just starve myself for a while — that should keep her happy. I may drink as much water as I want, eat as many fruits and vegetables as I can deal with, and that's about it. Goodbye double chocolate brownies with mocha frosting. Goodbye macadamia nut caramel popcorn.

Mom even downloaded the Calorie Count app onto her phone and onto mine. Now whenever we're calculating the calories, she pulls out her phone and looks up the foods. I accidentally leave my phone on my dresser pretty much every day. Oops, sorry, Mom, couldn't use the app at lunch, I forgot my phone. I don't mind leaving it at home; no one except my parents texts or calls anyway. My parents are my life. I have no other.

"This is Chelsea's life," Dad says. "Personally, I feel that if the doctor sees no health concerns, then Chelsea is absolutely perfect the way she is."

Dad gives me a big wink, and a surge of love almost chokes me.

Mom swivels on her feet and marches out of the kitchen. Her tan pants flash through the doorway and are gone. Dad thumps through the house, and I can hear him sink into his La-Z-Boy.

I extract a small tub of low-fat yogurt from the fridge and eat it slowly, taking two cauliflower stickers and placing them on my chart.

Fourteen

The WYP, or What's Your Problem?, club at school has asked me to join, but I have never in my life asked anyone what his or her problem is. If someone looks at me funny, if someone makes fun of me, instead of getting into his or her face, I flush a deep red and break out into a rash. I'm not like the WYP members.

"Hey, you," one of them shouts at me when I walk through the middle of the cafeteria. All of the members sit at the same table and talk as loudly as possible. Brandy is the ringleader and she scares me. She's more than six feet tall, looks like a Viking, and probably weighs about as much as my dad — somewhere in the three-hundred-pound category. Everyone is afraid to look at her because she's confrontational. Always.

"What's your problem?" she shouts at a cute girl who tries to get around her. "Find somewhere else to walk. I'm standing here. Don't even try to argue with me. You've got nothing to say to me. Go on. Get out of here."

When she turns her eyes back on me, I pretend that I have fifty friends on the other side of the cafeteria who are all waiting for me. I run across the room while stretching a smile onto my face and acting as if she doesn't bother me. If I had remembered to bring it, I could dig out my phone and pretend to be talking into it.

"You got a problem with me?" she calls after me. "You have to run away from me whenever I'm talking to you? Yeah, I'm talking to you. You know it. I've seen you."

I'm perfectly aware that she's talking to me, but I don't know how to respond to her. She's beautiful, strong, and unintimidated. I take a different route through the cafeteria tables, moving away from her, slinking past a table of gamers who are talking about something called the Vault of Glass.

"I know you try to hide, setting your ass down in the corners, trying to cover your beauty with sweaters and jeans. Squeeze that body into something sexy. Let the world see what you've got. Why are you so quiet and bashful?" She's practically shouting this, but hardly anyone pays attention. This is pretty typical Brandy.

I sit down at a table two rows over from her, but she's still talking to me. It's not as if I don't like what she has to say — I would like to stand up for myself, wear beautiful clothes that match my beautiful shoes, but every time I try, the rash flashes across my arms, down my legs, even onto my feet, and I can't talk.

I immediately get up again because a girl named Eva and a group of her friends are crowding me out.

"Don't let those girls take over your table and make you move. Get up in their face and ask them what their problem is." I wish she wouldn't talk so loudly. I wish she'd talk to someone else.

I have to slip past Brandy again. I avoid eye contact, but can feel her looking at me, turning her body to follow me, putting her hands on her hips to send me a message.

I walk out of the cafeteria and sit in the hallway to eat my lunch. I can't do it. I don't talk like the WYPs. I don't flaunt like them. I'm not confident like them. Attention makes my insides flutter and twist, flip and turn. Please notice someone else, someone who won't melt like snow in the heat.

Fifteen

Bridgette leads our Calorie Counters meetings. I still like her, but I know she sees through my facade. I can tell that she doesn't like the safe smile I give her — she knows what's really behind it.

At our first group gathering, she tells us her story. When we walk into the main meeting area, light glows from a projector set up in the back of the room. It projects a picture of a very large woman holding a baby. The woman's long and stringy hair falls around her shoulders. It looks like it needs to be washed. I can't relate to the woman. I don't have a child. I'm not that large. I always wash my hair.

"This was me," Bridgette says.

I jolt up in my seat and catch my smile before it jumps off my face. I would never in a million years guess that Bridgette and this woman were even related.

"Ten years ago, I weighed three hundred pounds. As you can see, I have big bones, I'm tall, I can carry that weight around, but it certainly hampered my life."

She changes the slide. In the next picture, she is seated at the edge of a pool in tight shorts and a purple tank top, which appear to be her version of a swimsuit. She grins at the camera over her shoulder while one hand steadies the plastic floatation device holding the baby.

"I couldn't fly on airplanes without paying for a first class seat, and I couldn't go to the movie theater without sitting in a special chair in the back," Bridgette says. "I couldn't walk around in public without being stared at."

She flips to the next slide, which shows her seated

on a brown couch, a toddler on her lap. They are reading a book together.

"My husband left me when Matt, our son, was two."

She clicks through more slides and tells her story. My mom watches with her mouth slightly open.

"Five years ago, I developed late-onset diabetes, which usually doesn't affect people until they're into their sixties or seventies. I was thirty-six years old." Bridgette looks around the room, ready for us to contradict her claim, to challenge her. None of us will, though; we know it's true. "I decided to change my life."

She clicks through pictures that show her shrinking in jumps and starts. At first the weight loss isn't clearly noticeable, but she's at a park with her son and both are laughing while spraying water from a drinking fountain. Then there's a picture where she's pulling the waist of a large pair of pants out, indicating inches of weight loss. Then she's in a navy-blue suit with the label *job interview* beneath the picture.

"After losing fifty pounds, my diabetes disappeared," she says.

I can tell that she feels better about herself in the newer pictures because her hair is clean and fashionably styled, and she is starting to look like the current Bridgette.

"After losing one hundred and twenty pounds, I treated myself to Paris."

In this picture, she stands near the Arc de Triomphe with a boy who looks like he's about eight, and a James Bond-looking man — tall, debonair, and mustached. He has his arm around her.

"And now, I have a new life," she says. She turns off the projector, hits the lights, and walks to the front of the room. The metal folding chair creaks underneath me. Mom squeezes my bumpy-rashed arm. I'm worried that she'll want to hold my hand, but she just squeezes and withdraws.

Bridgette is beautiful. I have a hard time reconciling her with the woman in those old photos. She looks so put together and in control. The woman in the pictures looked disheveled and dumpy.

"You can do the same," she says, looking each one of us in the eye. My mom smiles back like all this information is aimed at her even though she's skinnier than the current Bridgette. "And that is why we are all here."

I'm ready to leave. This is not for me. I'm not disheveled and frumpy. I am not that woman in the picture — my life is not controlled by my weight. I know what I want to do with my life, where I want to go, what I want to accomplish. I don't need this.

I almost get up and walk out right then, but trying to explain all this to Mom would be exhausting and she would not understand. I stay in my chair and listen to Bridgette discuss how she changed her eating habits and lifestyle so she could remain under two hundred pounds. My mom scribbles frantically in a small notebook she brought along while I try not to yawn.

Calorie Counters Meeting #2

Weight Loss: nada

Sixteen

Not only do I have to make an autobiography of myself for film as literature II, I have to volunteer my time at the Spring Fling dance. I do not attend school dances. I do not attend school functions. I stay home, do my homework, watch movies with my dad, sing to my favorite musicals, put nail polish on my toenails, and hide from the neighbor girls.

Mr. Butler informs us that he buys a new digital video camera every year for this class. In order to afford the camera, we have to raise money by putting on the Spring Fling dance. I'd like to fling the dance all right — into an active volcano somewhere.

Mr. Butler organizes us into groups:

refreshments

decorations

ticket taking and marketing

The date is already set, March thirteenth — a week before spring break. All we have to do as free labor is figure out what refreshments we need, how we'll decorate the gym, and then make some posters.

I sign up for the ticket sales and marketing committee, and so does the girl who sits beside me.

"Melody," she says, holding out her hand. Today she wears a white pirate shirt with a black vest over it. Her jeans are ragged cutoffs that extend just below the knees and her head is wrapped in a tight black bandana. I'm surprised she isn't wearing an eye patch.

Before I can reply she says, "Chelsea. I know."

Marcus Vemen, the kid I've gone to school with all my life, signs up for the same committee. He's short — really short — and makes up for it by trying to be funny.

"I'm surprised you didn't sign up for the refreshments committee," he says, then laughs really hard while looking around at the other guys in the group. One of them laughs, but everyone else looks at their desks or suddenly finds something very important to search for in their backpacks.

"What the hell is your problem?" Melody says, glaring right at him.

I have my safe smile fixed onto my face as I examine my fingernails, but when she says this I look up. Marcus and Melody glare at each other and crane their necks forward. Marcus is the first to back off. He shrugs and picks at something in his teeth. He makes sure his shaggy hair is curled around his ears and dripping into his eyes and then he glances back up at Melody.

"You," she says, pointing her finger at Marcus, "are in charge of finding out what time the dance starts, how much tickets have cost in the past, what our DJ choices are, and what our Spring Fling theme will be this year. Until Big Shit has all that figured out, we might as well figure out what week we should sign out the movie cameras."

She turns and looks at me.

"Let's sign up for different weeks so we can work together," she says. "You can film me; I'll film you. If you want."

I realize that I'm staring and quickly look away. I nod, once, and then wonder what I'm getting myself into. Like I want someone dressed as a pirate entering my life and helping me display myself on film. My safe smile has gone flat, so I tip the corners of my mouth up and nod.

She is signed up for the week of March fourth, the week before the big Spring Fling dance that is sure to become the bane of my existence, and I am signed up for the week of April twenty-second. At least I have a month to come up with some reason why she can't help me film myself — like maybe I have smallpox or malaria or mad cow disease, making it impossible for me to work cooperatively with someone and making it a bad idea for me to touch and possibly contaminate the video equipment.

Seventeen

I buy all my clothes online. My mom thinks that's crazy and still goes to the mall for day-long trips during which she tries on ninety outfits and purchases two. Why anyone would want to spend that much time on clothes is beyond me.

When I need a new pair of jeans, I go online. When

I need something fashionable to wear to a Spring Fling that I would rather not attend, I go online. I have been purchasing my bras online since I was ten years old.

I'm pretty sure that I was the only girl in my fourth grade class to get her period. Okay, maybe Marjorie Vries got her period that year too; we avoided each other because we were about the same size and couldn't acknowledge that fact to each other or our classmates. For all I know, Marjorie Vries is my soul mate, but I'll never find out because we still don't talk and we keep away from each other in English.

The day I got my first period, I thought I was dying. I had no idea that females bled. My mother had not had the talk with me yet. I had a pretty good idea where babies came from and how men were involved with their personal equipment, but I didn't know about bleeding, periods, tampons, and pads.

I'd been at school, feeling achy, feverish, and clammy, and when I went to the bathroom because I felt like I'd leaked some pee into my underwear, I practically fainted. No pee in my underwear. Blood. I was dying.

I called my mom at work. She came to pick me up, and we headed straight over to see Dr. Lawrence. My mom had assumed that she still had years before she needed to tell me about the facts of life. She hadn't gotten her period until she was fourteen. Her daughter was physically an adult at the age of ten? There was something seriously wrong.

Dr. Lawrence presented me with all the juicy menstrual cycle nuances. She even put her arm around my shoulders and said, "Many overweight girls get their periods early. We're not sure why that is, but it does seem to be a common occurrence."

I hated her. I hated my mom for not warning me about pads, tampons, and menstrual cycles. I loved my dad because when Mom and I got home from the doctor's office, he bought me clam chowder and ice cream, which we ate together while watching *10 Things I Hate About You*, supposedly some Shakespeare rip-off. (Dad never would have watched it otherwise.) He fell asleep about halfway through the movie, but I still loved him for sitting there with me. Even though I could now physically procreate, I was still his little girl.

Eighteen

Now that Nicholas Dunn knows my name, he thinks we're friends.

"Hey, Chubby Chelsea," he says. Accounting has not quite begun yet, and I'm wishing that he would just turn around so I can stare at the back of his head, which is much more attractive and friendly than the front. "You like ice cream? You like pork rinds? You like big fat tubs of lard?" He whispers this to me; the words come out in sticky clumps full of Nicholas Dunn saliva. "I'll bet you eat butter straight out of the wrapper. Big old fatty cubes of butter. Potato chips. What kind do you like? Ruffles? Pringles? Lays? You dip them in that cheesy dip or French onion?"

I will not look at Nicholas Dunn. I stare down at my accounting workbook, dreaming I could destroy him with the lasers that shoot from the top of my head. I can't get my safe smile to stay on my face; it keeps slipping away. I blink. I swallow hard. Ms. Sandell stands at the front of the room trying to get our attention, trying to distract Nicholas Dunn, who apparently believes that it is his mission in life to make me feel like a wart.

I can't stand Nicholas Dunn. I know you're not supposed to hate people, but I have a very difficult time not hating him. I don't know why. He's nothing new. There has been a Nicholas Dunn every year of my life. In third grade it was Stephanie Burger, who made me pull down my underwear and show her my butt in the bathroom. In fourth grade it was Elaine Turner, who would poke her finger into my stomach as far as it would go and claim that I kept my lunch money tucked between my folds of fat. In fifth grade it was Tanner Swift, who pretended that I was causing an earthquake when I walked down the hallway. In sixth grade it was Marcus Vemen, who would run into me on purpose and then bounce across the hallway, making his friends laugh so hard they'd have to lean against each other. Marcus Vemen and his inability to mature still does this, when he has the opportunity. Nicholas Dunn is nothing new. All the tormentors are the same. All their faces melt into one.

When I get home from school that day, I find a new batch of double chocolate mocha frosting brownies, and because mom isn't home to tell me how many Calorie Count points are in a brownie, I eat three and then curl up in front of the TV to watch Ellen DeGeneres.

I haven't painted my toenails in two weeks. It is time for a new coat.

Calorie Counters Meeting #3

Weight Loss: zero

Weight Gain: two pounds

Nineteen

After our Calorie Counters meeting, Mom avoids asking me how much my weigh-in was. She knows that it's secret and that we're not supposed to tell each other, but after every visit, she "confides" in me about her own weight and tonight is no different.

"Another pound lost, Chelsea. I only have three more to go to meet my optimal weight." She pats me on the shoulder and smiles her horsey smile.

We get in the car, and I take my time buckling my seat belt.

"I'm sure you're just as successful as I am." She pats my knee and then puts the car into reverse. I tuck my hands under my legs and think about those two pounds gained. It must have been the yogurt, or perhaps the brownies I ate after the yogurt, or maybe the popcorn I ate after everyone else went to bed. Pretty sure there's no sticker for macadamia nut caramel popcorn.

Mom probably suspects that my weight loss isn't quite what it should be, because the next morning she imposes her new workout regimen on me.

"No more driving to work or school. From now on we ride our bikes."

I don't even try to grumble. Instead I go back inside, put my raincoat on, my backpack underneath, and come back out. Three miles to school — I can do this.

For the first week, mom rides her bike every day, but riding a bike in Oregon in the spring is like riding through a tsunami. Her pants get big mud splatters on them, so she takes a clean set of clothes in a backpack. But by the time she gets to work they're wrinkled, and my mom does not wear wrinkled clothes.

The next week she walks every day. It takes her forty-five minutes to walk to work. By the end of the week, she has blisters on her feet and is soaking them in Epsom salt at night. The third week, she starts driving again.

I bike to school. Every day. I try to tell Mom that it won't make a difference; when I start working out a lot, I gain weight; I don't lose it. I think it has something to do with muscle weighing more than fat, but I don't mind riding my bike. The rain feels good on my face, the earthworm smell makes me think of flowers, and the breeze wakes me up.

I wear my yellow slicker, flip-flops, and mittens. It takes me about twenty minutes to bike to school. I ride in the bike lane all the way, and join the other Oregon environmentalists in our united goal of fixing the ozone layer. Okay, so my reasons for biking to school aren't quite so noble, but at least I'm biking.

Our school squats low to the ground; it was erected in the seventies, which is really obvious because the outside is painted lime green, the insides are white, and half of the classroom walls are moveable so we can push the walls aside and join classes together for some new educational experience. I've never had a single teacher move the wall aside. It also appears that the construction crew forgot about the gym the first time around. It is connected to the school at one end only, and even though it could share a wall with one of the classrooms, it doesn't. There is a narrow alleyway between the gym and the main building. The whole school could use a makeover from a demolition company, but due to lack of school funding and apathy, I suspect students will be attending an outdated, ugly school for many years to come.

I park my bike in the bike racks by the gym, right next to the narrow walkway between the gym and the main building. Stoners and druggies use that space to support their habit, and they call the crevice "The Achievement Gap." I'm so used to seeing the same guys getting high in there that we nod acknowledgement when we see one another.

"Yo," a stoner-regular says.

I recognize this guy, but I've never actually seen him

in the school or in any of my classes. Maybe he takes correspondence courses channeled through his joint. I give him my careful smile.

"You've got yourself one hell of a sturdy cruiser there," he says.

I nod, but I can feel my smile fade. The problem with stoners is that they say stupid things, but they say them so sincerely and with so little malicious intent, that it's hard to get seriously offended. Does he really think I need some sort of a specially reinforced bike? Do I look that huge to him?

"It's just a bike," I say.

He nods, his eyes half closing, as if I've just revealed the meaning of life to him.

"As you were," he says, salutes, and slides back into The Achievement Gap.

Twenty

One day in the cafeteria, I almost sit down right beside Trevor Laats.

Trevor Laats is gorgeous and no one but me has

55

figured it out. I watch him all the time. He sits by himself in the cafeteria perusing these magazines about movies. He is way into movies, and when Mr. Butler said that we would be making autobiographies, he sat right up in his seat and took off his glasses to clean them.

That's his way of showing excitement.

He dresses like no other guy I've ever seen. He wears capris — seriously — short pants that extend just past his knees. They're not jeans either; they're khakis or lederhosen, or something. Then he wears these argyle vests that must have gone out of style about fifty years ago. Underneath the vests, he wears white button-up shirts with only the very top button left open. But most importantly, he wears flip-flops every single day, and he has the most beautiful feet I've ever seen. They're not hairy troll feet like my dad's and they're not bony witch feet like my mom's; they're long, slender, well-groomed feet with perfectly trimmed nails.

I can't be sure of the color of his eyes yet since I'm afraid to look him in the face, but I'm sure they're beautiful too; they would be beautiful, anyway, if he could just figure out how to keep his glasses from fogging up all the time.

The day when I almost sit down with him, he is reading his regular movie magazine and is camped out in the corner of the room in his typical spot. I slip over to his table and am about to sit down when someone knocks into my tray. I juggle frantically, trying to re-secure my grip before milk, grilled cheese sandwich, and tomato soup slop all over the place, but I'm too slow. The whole mess goes on my shirtfront, down my pants, and onto my feet. Three little freshmen, all laughing so hard they're about to pee in their pants, run away from me.

Crouching to the floor, I scoop up what I can of the food and put it back on my tray. A janitor comes bustling over, pushes me aside, and mops at the mess with a washcloth. I back away. When I turn around, Trevor stands in front of me, half of a grilled cheese sandwich in hand, and gives it to me.

I cannot summon my safe smile but glance up into his face. He shoves his glasses up on his nose and squints at me.

"You okay?" he asks.

All I can do is look down at my tomato soup-encrusted shoes and wish that aliens would suck me up in their ship to do some testing.

"That's my little brother," he says. "He's an asshole."

Trevor isn't looking at me anymore. He's looking out into the cafeteria where three short freshmen with shaggy hair and baggy pants are pointing at me and laughing. I wonder what it must be like for Trevor to live in a house with an icky little freshman boy who dares to pick on a sophomore and not have any regrets or qualms.

After lunch I go home. How am I supposed to sit in film class, staring at Trevor's beautiful feet with both of us trying to ignore the fact that I smell like a garbage can and it's all his brother's fault?

I add Trevor to my list of decent people in this world. That means I have a total of three people on my list. Dad, Bridgette, and Trevor Laats.

Twenty-one

Melody spots me in the hallway as I make my way to earth science. When she shouts out my name, I am so stunned that I stop right where I am and three people bump into me. Never stop in the middle of a high school hallway; it's like parking your car on a train track.

Today Melody looks like Peter Pan. She wears a green shirt/skirt type of outfit with black leggings. Her shoes are the same color as her outfit, and a jaunty little hat on her head completes the ensemble. She could have stepped through a window into Wendy's nursery.

"Chelsea," she pants as she catches up with me. "It's my week for the video camera already. You have to come over on Saturday. I have my entire wardrobe picked out. I know exactly what I want filmed. All we have to do is film it and then edit it. What time can you come over?"

I realize that my smile is gone, my eyebrows are furrowed, and that people are pushing around us to get to class. I also realize that I sound like a perfectly normal teenager — someone who is invited to a friend's house to work on a class project. Isn't that what teenagers do?

And then I come back down to earth and realize that the only reason she is inviting me over is because she needs someone to hold the video camera.

My careful smile is back, and I find out I can speak.

"Saturday, sure. Afternoon?"

"How about three?" she says. "Afterward we can order a pizza and watch a movie. I'll text you my number. What's yours?" Melody pulls out her phone and types my number in so quickly, I'm pretty sure she put in all fives. When she sends me her number in a text reply, I stare at it for a full twenty seconds. I know people do this; casually text one another their numbers, add the number to their contacts like Melody just did, but this is brand new to me. I'm scared that if I put my phone in my pocket her number will disappear, vanish, turn into obnoxious text gibberish like 2G2BT or FUBAR.

She shoves a card into my hand. There is no pirate or Peter Pan on the front of the card. Instead, there are

Japanese comic book characters. I've seen these figures before, but I've never really been into anime, so it's somewhat new to me. Her name, Melody Smiles, is printed near the bottom with her address right below her name. She has a business card for some reason, and it includes her e-mail address, cell phone number, and Twitter handle.

Maybe I should get my own card. Something with shoes on the front. Something with shoes and beautiful feet.

I can't help it; all through earth science I grin a full-on smile and swallow little happy bubbles that creep into my mouth and nose. I stick my hand into the pocket of my jeans and wrap my fingers around my phone, or feel the card that Melody gave me. My rash is back in full force, prickling across my arms and chest, but other than that I'm normal. Almost.

Twenty-two

My little happy bubbles don't last. After school, as I lean over my bike trying to unlock the chain, I hear a voice behind me and immediately feel clammy and can tell that my anxiety rash is rushing across my chest and up my neck yet again, like an unstoppable tidal wave.

"Chubby Chelsea," the voice says. "What a fine view you have given us."

I take my time — unlock the chain and wrap it around the neck of my bike seat. I turn slowly, careful to organize my lips into a tight smile and view the assholes taking in the view. Nicholas Dunn and two of his weightlifting buddies stand behind me flexing their pecs. I balance my bike against my leg and put on my helmet.

"That wide ass of yours is something else," Nicholas Dunn says, and his friends laugh. I press my lips tightly together, willing my smile to stay on my face.

"At least you can see your feet when you're biking," he says. The friend beside him laughs so hard he farts. They're blocking my way. I think about locking up my bike again and returning to the school, but I won't escape by doing that. I'll just trap myself further. I take a deep breath and try to still my thumping heart. Wheeling my bike around them, I move past the bike racks and out into the parking lot.

"Give me a ride, Chubby Chelsea," he yells at me. I do not turn to look at him. He runs to catch up with me, places a hand against my handlebars, and blocks my way. Then he jumps onto my handlebars and sits there, squashing my woven basket. I try really hard to keep my smile pulled tight, but I'm pretty sure I've got a grimace going and the tendons in my neck are popping out. My face feels so hot and flushed. I might burst blood vessels in my eyes.

"Bike me around, girlfriend," he says, and balances himself on the handlebars while waving his arms and legs in the air. "You think you can wheel us both around? Can your bike handle that much weight?"

My hands shake from the added load of Nicholas Dunn on my bike. Would it be so bad to just let go and run? That would mean leaving my bike here and having to make it home on foot. I need my bike. I need other options. I wish I was under my blanket and Nicholas Dunn would get trampled by wild boars. His friends laugh and block my way out of the parking lot, but I'm not going anywhere since I can't manage the unwanted passenger. My mouth feels suddenly dry and I have the urge to cough, but I worry that I'll lose my grip and drop the bike to the ground. I lick my lips instead. Nicholas Dunn hops down and stands in front of my bike, pushing against the handlebars, his hands hot against my own. His face is inches from mine. I can't back up, I can't let go of the handlebars, and I can't pull the bike out of his grip.

He leans in toward me and waggles his tongue in my face. He smells like musky cologne and hair gel.

I breathe faster and suck in my tears. I will not cry in front of him. He can't have that kind of control over me. I can feel the rash rushing across my chest, up my neck, down my arms. I can't speak or think or make any sense of this moment. How did I get here? Why is he doing this to me?

And then one of his friends touches him on the arm and says, "Clark." Nicholas Dunn suddenly lets go and casually moves between some parked cars to a small dark blue Jetta. Principal Clark comes from the back door of the school, walks past the bike racks, walkie-talkie in hand, and gives me his salesman smile. He has no idea who I am. He has no idea what Nicholas Dunn was saying to me, but at that moment, I love him with all my being and envision him with a sun halo around his head. Principal Clark, inadvertent savior. I consider adding him to my decent people list, but his decency was accidental.

I rub my face with my right hand, shakily hanging onto the bike with the other. I tremble everywhere; even my hair flutters around my face in wispy strands. I'm okay. I'm all right. I'll survive.

As I peddle home, I take my time. My muscles still shake, making my bike wobble precariously, but the farther I get from school, the more in control I feel. The sun is out in patches, and I feel the warmth of sunshine on my arms as the sleeves to my cotton shirt inch up my

63

wrists. The scent of Nicholas Dunn is still in my nose, and the heat of his hands against mine still burns. The breath of the wind against my fingers cools as I ride, and I hope to blow away Nicholas Dunn from my hands and from my mind. I think instead about Melody. What will we say to each other? We barely even know each other. What if I can't think of anything to say? I don't talk much as it is; in my family, Mom does the talking. She doesn't like quiet moments so she fills them in with just about anything. Dad says it's because she has an addictive personality and right now she's addicted to order, structure, and noise. He claims that's better than alcohol, which is what her mom was addicted to and is what her father and two sisters still live for.

But I'm not addicted to noise unless you count the musicals and singing. Okay, so that's noise, but I'm not addicted to talking and communicating. I could easily not say anything to anyone all night long and be perfectly happy. What if Melody doesn't like quiet? Hopefully she'll know how to fill it if I'm not able to do my part.

Twenty-three

Our assignment for Calorie Counters was to bring in a favorite recipe — one that is low in fat and doesn't use more than four Calorie Count points — to share with the group.

Mom brings in this recipe for Indian rice. She's never made it before, but it's low in fat and looks good. We don't do a lot of cooking at our house unless you consider opening a box cooking. We make rice from a box, spaghetti sauce from a jar, soup from a can, and full dinners from microwaveable containers. I'm pretty sure those are the four food groups: box, jar, can, container.

I bring in a recipe for Caesar salad. I've even made it before. Twice. It was pretty good, but not great.

When we get to Calorie Counters, Bridgette and I go into the pastel torture chamber to stand on the pink scale. I have gained two pounds. Bridgette backs away from the scale and sits in the pastel blue chair. She points to the other chair and I sit beside her.

"Chelsea," she says. Her hand is under her chin and she leans against it. I summon my careful smile and rub my hands together in my lap. I'm glad my mother isn't in the room. She has successfully lost all of her weight, and they've told her not to come to the meetings anymore. She insists on coming, though, for moral support. I'm not sure who she's supporting, though, because it sure isn't me.

Bridgette is waiting for me to speak first. I know what she wants me to say; that I'm not ready for this, that I jumped into the program too early, that I'm not doing this for me. What comes out of my mouth is not what I expected to say.

"I don't want to lose weight."

She bites her lower lip, raises her eyebrows, and nods. I stick a finger in my mouth and start to chew on the nail.

"I mean I want to lose weight, I know I should lose weight for my health and everything, but I don't really feel like losing weight. I don't feel like taking on the whole program and forcing myself to count all these little points and then wishing I could be thin like my mom. I'm not thin. I'm not built like my mom. I don't really care that I'm heavier than she is, I mean, that's fine with me."

"Whoa," Bridgette says, sitting back in her chair and holding up the hand that had been supporting her chin. "Does it matter to you that other people notice how heavy you are?"

"Well, yeah." I take a deep breath. "I mean, it

matters that my mom's worried about my weight and it matters that people call me names and stuff, but I kind of like who I am. I think I'm an okay person, and I don't understand why people call me names or why they don't like me just because I'm overweight. Why is it so terrible for someone to be a little overweight?"

"Honey," she says, leaning forward in her chair. "People should like you for who you are. Your weight shouldn't matter and I'm glad that you like who you are. But are you telling me that you are not bothered by the fact that others don't see beyond size?"

"Yeah, kind of," I say and shrug. "But that's not my problem — that's their problem. They should see beyond size and like me for who I am. I mean, did it bother you that your husband left you because you were overweight?"

"Howard didn't deserve me," Bridgette says. She sits up straight and raises her chin. "He didn't know what he had."

"Was he the reason you wanted to lose weight?"

"He made me realize that if I loved myself, I should have respect for myself and take better care of my body."

I nod but I don't really understand.

"Why didn't you discover that you loved and respected yourself when you were still married to him? Why did he have to leave for you to feel that way?

Why does it have to be the opinion of others that matters so much?"

"Sometimes we have to hit an all-time low before we decide that we should change ourselves. Maybe you haven't hit the all-time low yet."

I stand up, fold my arms over my chest, and look down at Bridgette.

"You know, if the world around me wasn't fixated on weight, I wouldn't be either," I say, feeling my cheeks begin to flush. "The world around me needs to change, not me."

Bridgette nods, stands, and extends her hand. We shake.

"Maybe another time, Chelsea, or maybe never if you're able to change the world."

We walk out into the waiting room, where my mother is waiting. Mom stands up when she sees us, her recipe card in hand.

"Come on, Mom," I say and walk out the door.

It takes her a few seconds, but she follows me.

"Where are you going?" she asks, her voice high.

"Home."

"But you haven't achieved your optimal weight," she says, running to catch up with me.

"You have," I say. "That's all that really matters."

She grabs my arm and whirls me around.

"Chelsea Duvay, when are you going to have some respect for yourself? When are you going to face the truth? You are overweight. For your own good, you need to reach your optimal weight."

Her fingers are strong, squeezing my arm. We're standing on the sidewalk outside the Calorie Counters clinic. A couple comes out of the Hallmark store, and they pretend they're not eavesdropping, but glance at us quickly, then look away. Mom and I are the same height. Our faces are inches apart, and I can see a fleck of spit on her lower lip. I can also see thin veins of red in the tired whites of her eyes.

"Mom, I have respect for myself. When are you going to have some respect for me?"

Neither of us says a word on the way home.

Calorie Counters Meeting #4

Weight Loss: zero

Weight Gain: two pounds

Twenty-four

I arrive early to Melody's house on Saturday, and bike around the block three times before going to the door. It's overcast, cloudy, cool, but it's not raining so I don't mind the ride. Melody lives about three miles away from me. My family lives in a new housing development with cloned houses that only differ in paint color. Melody lives in an old neighborhood full of ranch-style houses with huge trees growing all around them and a creek trickling through the backyards. It smells good there — like leaves, rain, and earthworms.

Even though I'm nervous, I know I'm at the right place and the right time because she's texted me sixteen times in the last three days. That's my new all-time record for texts received from a friend within a three-day window.

I lean my bike against the side of the garage and walk to the front door. I feel sweaty and hope I don't smell. She might second-guess our friendship if I ask to take a shower on my very first visit to her house. My smile is stuck to my face, and I test it out by inching the corners up just a bit. I dry my hands on my pants and ring the doorbell. I can feel the flush starting at my chest and spreading like fire.

She must have been waiting at the door. It opens immediately and Melody grabs my arm, pulling me in. I get a quick glimpse of a bare belly, and as I follow her down the hallway, the silk from her full skirt brushes against my legs and some filmy material from her shirt flies into my mouth. I cough.

"You have got to check out my wardrobe. I've chosen all the best outfits and have arranged them according to season. We'll start with summer, work our way through fall and winter, and end with spring. After every season I want to film some of my manga. I'll start with my early stuff and then work into my most recent pieces. I'm actually working on a graphic novel. Here."

She hands me the digital video camera while leading me through her house. They have knocked out most of the walls. The kitchen, dining room, living room, and family room are all one big room with posts and beams supporting the ceiling here and there. We rush through this monstrous main room, which is littered with cloth and patterns, and work our way to a hallway, which has four doorways leading off of it: the bathroom, an enormous closet, Melody's room, and another bedroom, which I assume is her parents'.

In Melody's room, a double four-poster bed with a canopy fills most of the space. A computer with graphic novels stacked all around it occupies the desktop and most of the back wall. She has a dresser, a small closet, and a chair. Anime posters, drawings, and artwork cover every inch of the walls. I feel like I have stepped into a different country, one with Japanese artwork, filmy material around the bed, and pounds and pounds of fabric.

"See, it's all laid out." Her hand sweeps over the bed where everything from black capes to tiaras overlap and drape across one another. I recognize the Peter Pan outfit, the pirate pants, and some of her punk-wear, but most of the outfits are new to me. "All you have to do is stand outside the door and film five seconds of me walking through the door with a different outfit on. I've got thirty outfits; seven for each season and a couple extras. This is who I am: hyper, ever-changing, versatile, and stylish. You ready?"

I look down at the camera in my hand. I know how to operate it. I know what's expected. I stick my smile on my face and meet her eyes.

"I'm ready," I say.

"Okay, you stand outside the front door. I'm already wearing my belly-dancing outfit, but after this one it will take me a few minutes to get changed."

"Right," I say.

I walk out of her bedroom, down the hallway, and through the kitchen/living room/dining room/family room to the front door, where I head outside and wait.

I have a real grin on my face as I stand in her front yard. In fact, I laugh out loud. I'd been so worried — what would I say to her, what would we talk about, but I realize now that she's not that type of person. Melody doesn't leave room for small talk — she gets right to business. I've got nothing to worry about.

I film her opening the door, stepping out onto the top step, gliding down onto the next step, and then down the path. She has a chain attached to her nose that goes all the way to her ear. She's beautiful, serene. When she has advanced down the walkway a few steps, she yells "cut."

We watch the five seconds of video that I recorded just then, which actually turn out to be eight seconds of video.

"Okay, my feet aren't on here. You've got to get my feet. Back up just a few steps," she says. "I know, why don't you go stand in the doorway and I'll figure out the right place for the video camera."

"You want me to stand in the doorway?"

"Yeah. I'll figure out the right angle so you get my haram slippers in the screen as well as my veil. Go stand in the doorway so I can figure this out."

I understand what she wants me to do, but I can't do it. If she films me, if she starts taping me standing in the doorway, I might not live and I will never, ever speak to her again. My heart pounds. My hands sweat. My feet have turned to stone as I drag them up the few steps to the front door. Even though my sweatshirt covers my arms, I know they are flushing with red Himalaya bumps. I had thought I was safe — I wouldn't have to come up with small talk — but it had never occurred to me that I might be filmed and see my obvious flaws caught forever on video.

She backs up into the grass on her lawn and I stand in the doorway to her house. I bite my bottom lip so hard I taste the iron nip of blood. What does she see when she looks through the viewfinder? Does she now see me for what I truly am, overweight and a social pariah? Will she remove my number from her phone and never text me again? She takes another step backward and shouts.

"Perfect. Take two," she says.

I have to steady myself against the door frame. I suck in deep breaths and slowly walk toward her as my heart calms. The rough rash runs up my arms like rabid chicken pox and I hope I don't faint right here in her yard. Carefully, I uncurl my hands and force my legs to unstick themselves and carry me forward.

"Stand here," she says, grabbing my arms and adjusting my position. "Okay, one more time."

She runs back into the house. I am breathing hard but trying to relax. The camera shakes in my hands. The bumps are still there and I wonder how obvious they are on my neck, on my cheeks, and across the top of my chest.

"Ready?" she asks.

I suck in a breath, close my eyes for a second, and then exhale. By holding my arm tight against my body, I can steady my hand.

"Ready," I say, my voice wobbling. I hope she doesn't notice.

She emerges from the house one more time. Her golden haram shoes are caught on camera as is the top of her head, which is barely discernible beneath the filmy fabric of the veil. It's perfect.

Two and a half hours later, we have filmed all of her outfits. I'm not shaking. I'm not biting my lip. I'm not even attached to my frozen smile anymore. The red rash has receded, and I can't see it anymore on my arms. I realize that Melody just doesn't give a shit, and if she doesn't, why should I?

Twenty-five

My mom always tells me that the reason I am an only child is because my father's lack of maturity makes him a child as well. Why have more than two? My dad is goofy, fun, and off-the-wall, but my mother is more childish than he is.

For some unfathomable reason, she invites her obnoxious dad over for Easter dinner even though it's a train wreck every year. Maybe she sees this as her duty, trying to make up for some deficit in her life. She's a good Irish-Catholic girl who never goes to church anymore and certainly doesn't have a personal connection with God unless you count using his name in vain, but she continues to resurrect Christmas and Easter traditions that feel empty and trite.

Two years ago on Easter, Mom invited Grandpa Reece over for dinner, and he showed up drunk as usual. I used to think that he smelled so spicy because he used too much aftershave lotion, but as I got older, I figured out that his overuse of aftershave lotion was intentional; he was trying to cover up another smell, the one that reminded me of those guys on the city bus who either slump in their seats or shout out sentences that don't make any sense. "I didn't eat it!" "Whose pants are these?!" Grandpa Reece swears just as much as those guys do. If I said the "F" word at the dinner table, my mother would roll over dead. All she does is grimace and try to change the subject when he says it.

When I opened the door for him that year at Easter, he wrapped his arms around me and squeezed. Then he grabbed handfuls of flesh at my waist and shouted, "You get more than a handful with this girl, don't you?"

Then he laughed so hard, his ever-pink nose turned scarlet. I went to my room, tried to control my shaking limbs and raging rash, and didn't come out until he was gone. I tried to calm myself, but I could think about nothing except all the times he had embarrassed me.

The worst had been when I was really young, probably in first or second grade. I'd gone to the park with Grandpa. We'd gone down the slide, swung on the swings, and whirled on the merry-go-round. Then he put me on the teeter-totter. He thought he'd created quite the amusing math problem. He found four kids and tried to figure out what combination of the four would balance with me on the teeter-totter. We ended up with me on one side and brothers who looked two or three years younger than me on the other. That was right around the time that I figured out about being isolated, unaccepted, tormented, and stared at. Overweight people are modern-day lepers. Don't get too close to us, you might catch what we've got.

77

That particular Easter two years ago, when Grandpa Reece finally left and dinner was over, I came out of my room and sat in the living room on the couch. I was done being mad and pounding my fists into my bed. I was done crying, storming, and singing to myself. My rash had become a mere hint along my collarbones. I haven't spoken to Grandpa Reece since.

Dad sat in his regular La-Z-Boy with Mom in his lap. He wrapped his big bear arms around her and she pressed her face into his neck. He rocked back and forth, humming, and I sat on the couch. I don't remember what was on TV, but I remember the song my dad was singing. It was a song from *Fiddler on the Roof* — "Gentle, kind and affectionate, the sweet little bird you were, Chavala, Chavala." I hummed along with him and rocked myself on the couch. I guess being overweight isn't the only thing in the world that can mess with your self-esteem.

Twenty-six

When I was in fourth grade I not only got my first period, I had to get braces on my teeth. No one in my class but me had braces, just like no one in my class

78

but me knew how to use a tampon. I was practically Albert Einstein.

When I came home from the orthodontist with shiny new braces that cut into my lips and made my jaw ache, Dad was waiting. He opened the door to the house — threw it open when I walked up the path — and stood there grinning. He had a metal coat hanger strapped around his face, bent so it pushed against his teeth, and he kept throwing his arms in the air and stomping around while singing his own version of "Macho Man" as loudly as he could.

"Gancho, gancho man. I want to be a gancho man."

He told me later that *gancho* means "hook" in Spanish. He didn't know what the Spanish word for hanger was. Hook was the best he could do.

I swore I wouldn't smile until my braces were gone, removed, recycled into the shape of a toaster or maybe a car fender, but when Dad kept jumping around, shaking the floor and singing "Gancho Man" at the top of his lungs, I couldn't help but smile. By the end of the night he had me laughing so hard, I could barely open my mouth the next day. My mouth and jaw ached so much.

Sometimes when I'm depressed, Dad will get out that coat hanger and do a reenactment of his "Gancho Man" performance. It still makes me laugh.

Twenty-seven

We film Melody in her thirty outfits and then head back inside the house. She wants to watch the video right away, but before positioning herself on the bed, she brings me into the room that I had mistaken for a closet.

"Anytime you ever want to borrow an outfit for Halloween or Christmas or just to wear to school, come on over. Help yourself to anything in here."

I follow Melody into the closet, which turns out to be a huge room with rows and rows of costumes. There is a whirring sound coming from behind the three-way mirror in the back that I assume is some sort of ventilation system that keeps the air circulating so the clothes don't get musty. Staring at all those outfits, I laugh out loud. I can't help it. This is where I can find the main characters from all my favorite musicals: Elphaba Thropp from *Wicked*, Fantine from *Les Misérables*, Annie from, well, *Annie*. Melody, still in her last outfit from filming, walks up and down the rows in leopard skin tights, a pink wig, and a black leather jacket. She walks with her hand out, feeling all the costumes, and I follow her doing the same. My fingers touch rough webbing, silks, cashmere, mosquito netting, cotton, and nylon all in the space of a few feet. I want to bury my face in an angora sweater and breathe in the depth of all these personas. I could be whatever I wanted in this room — lose myself in crepe de chine or silk. I could morph into beauty — draped in queenly robes, encased in silk, feathered in boas.

Melody is gone — watching her video — and I start pulling the costumes out to examine them.

Gingham dresses from the era of Laura Ingalls Wilder look fun, but I can tell right away they won't fit me. I find a biker outfit of black leather that's tempting to try on, but I worry about stretching the material. Then I find THE costume. I remove the hanger from the bar with caution and suck in my breath when I see what I have. I make my way to the three-way mirror behind the racks while holding the long black material against me. When I stand in front of the mirror, I know it will fit. I don't have to remove any of my own clothes; I just drape the black robe over top of my sweatshirt and jeans and let it fall to the floor. Then I pull the hood up, and slip on the mask.

I stare at myself in the mirror.

I know I should sing the part of the Phantom, but whenever Dad and I watch the movie, I sing the part of Christine while he becomes the Phantom. And immediately, the song's lyrics float into my head:

And do I dream again for now I find

The Phantom of the Opera is there

Inside my mind

I close my eyes and sway, repeating the lines again and again. At this moment, I am Christine. I am wrapped in another time, another body, someone else's reality. I am the star of the show and the Phantom supports me always, causing disaster when Carlotta tries to take my glory away from me. I am famous, revered, and honored everywhere, and when my beautiful voice rings through the auditorium, the audience cries, laughs, gasps, and responds how I desire it to respond. The lyrics flit through my mind again and then I bite down on my tongue. I realize that something has changed around me and I am back in the present, my own body, my own life. Imperfections.

The sound of the fan has stopped and without the background whir, the room is silent.

I open my eyes.

A face peers out at me from behind the three-way mirror. It looks like Melody's face, but not quite. The eyes are different — smoky blue and dark. Melody's eyes are light blue, with flecks of cloud in them. These eyes are surrounded by tiny creases that stretch up into the eyebrows, down into the cheeks, and out toward the hairline.

"Sorry, I didn't mean to stop you," the face says.

I realize that I am holding my breath. My hands are clutching at the material around my chest, bunching and squeezing. I relax my hands and exhale.

"Stop what?" I ask, my voice cracking.

"Your singing. It was marvelous. I really felt like I was there — that you were Christine. But I see now that you're not Christine — you're the Phantom."

"I'm the Phantom," I repeat.

She stares at me for another minute, searching for my eyes, and I remember the mask. She can't see how red my face is, how fluttery my insides feel, how sweaty I have become in the past five seconds.

"If I go back to sewing, will you sing again?" she asks after a minute.

I swallow. "I don't think I can," I say.

She laughs and all those creases sweep her eyes up into wings.

"Don't mind me, I'm just the elf behind the mirror."

"You made all these clothes?" I ask, my hand emerging from the black robe to sweep over the thousands of outfits lining the room.

"Well, a few of them I purchased, or bought pieces for, but most of them are made by hand."

I suck in my breath. Then I hear the sound of combat boots marching down a row.

"Chelsea, this sucks. We have to redo the one where I'm General Ann Dunwoody. My hat was on backward and all you can see of my face is a huge shadow." Melody puts one hand on her hip and waves with the other. "Hi, Mom."

Melody holds the video camera. She has already changed into the General Ann Dunwoody outfit. (Before today I'd never even heard of General Ann Dunwoody. I'd never heard of a lot of people Melody dresses up as. Anne Bonney? Kristine Lilly? Jacqueline Cochran?) While Melody stands between me and the mirror, and beside her mom, I see again how much they look alike. Aside from the eyes, they could be twins. They both have puffy bottom lips that make them look a bit pouty and cute noses that are turned up slightly at the end.

"I was just listening to Chelsea," Melody's mom says.

"Was she singing?" Melody asks, looking at me, or actually at my mask. "She does that all the time."

"I do not," I say.

"All the time," Melody says, opening her eyes wide and raising her eyebrows. "Why do you think I never talk to you in class? You're always singing, and it sounds so good, I just want to listen."

I am so glad I have the mask on. She can't see the sweat breaking out under my nose — the red of my face turning scarlet — my biting my bottom lip. Gah. I've been singing in front of Trevor. What must he think of me? I don't want to tell her that she talks constantly; she rarely listens.

"Come on," Melody says. She grabs my wrist and pulls me behind her. When I hear the start of the sewing machine, which I'd thought was a fan, I turn around and glance behind me. The elf is gone.

Twenty-eight

We watch musicals whenever Grandma and Grandpa Duvay come over. I've seen *Fiddler on the Roof, Grease, The Phantom of the Opera*, and *Les Misérables* about ten thousand times. I know all the lyrics to the songs.

This last year at Christmas, Grandma and Grandpa Duvay came over and we watched *Fiddler on the Roof.* I took the part of the daughters — whenever they had a solo, I sang along. Grandma did the mother, Dad did the father, and Grandpa was the fiddler. He really does fiddle and can play the song exactly like the fiddler in the movie. In the summer, when they travel over from eastern Oregon for the Fourth of July, we sit on the back deck and Grandpa fiddles. Sometimes Dad will get up and do a jig and we'll all laugh as he stumbles about red-faced.

Mom sits and listens. She'll smile occasionally, but she can't sing and doesn't even try.

Whenever we watch the musical and it is my turn to sing, Grandma throws her arm over my shoulders and pulls me against her. She's like a cotton pillow — spongy and comfortable with her inviting arms, soft sides, and lack of accusations. She always smells like molasses: sugary, sweet molasses with a dusting of ginger.

We tried to have Grandpa Reece come over for Christmas one time with Grandma and Grandpa Duvay, but he kept commenting about how he felt like a carrot on a pumpkin farm. When he said that for the fourth time, Grandma Duvay said to him in her retired librarian voice, "Now Reece, some of our foibles cause us to be bitter and nasty while others give us strength and character."

I don't think he knew what foibles meant, but he didn't say anything about the fat farm after that. He also couldn't sing, just like my mom. She hums, all the time, to whatever tune is playing in her head. Usually I can't recognize the tune she's humming.

When Melody tells me that I sing all the time, I begin to be aware of it. She's right. I sing in the shower, I sing when I ride my bike, I sing in film as literature II class.

I never, ever sing in accounting.

Twenty-nine

Nicholas Dunn has a girlfriend. She's in my film as literature II class, but sits near the front of the room. Sometimes I stare at the back of her head and try to figure out why any human being would go out with Nicholas Dunn. There must be something wrong with her — brain fever most likely. Or perhaps she has a bizarre disorder that causes her to only look at his face and well-muscled chest rather than seeing beyond the physical to his heart of asphalt. Oh right — that's not a bizarre disorder. It's an epidemic.

Her name is Eva McGuire. Not pronounced Eeeva, but Ayyva, like Ava Gardner. She's cute in a too-much-makeup sort of way. Her hair is long, super-long, and hangs down her back all the way to her butt. Before she sits down at her desk, she has to swish her light brown hair out of the way so she doesn't sit on it or smash it between her back and the chair's back. Her eyes are so lined in black that they make the rest of her face look exceptionally pale and her green eyes stand out. She also changes her lipstick color to match her clothes.

I feel like a swamp rat when I'm near her.

First semester we were both handing in our final essays to Mr. Butler's desk at the back of the room, and she bumped against me. I caught a quick whiff of Forbidden Euphoria or whatever Calvin Klein perfume she had on. I tried not to gag.

"Watch what you're doing," she said to me, her lips pursed into crabby lines.

I adjusted my smile and blinked.

She looked me up and down. I didn't mean to, but I glanced down at myself at the same time. I wore regular attire — sweatshirt, jeans, and open-toed shoes. She wore skintight black leggings, a blowsy pink shirt that flared at the waist but was tight around the boobs, and stilettos. She looked like a Disney princess.

"Shit," she said. "Have some respect for yourself."

My smile never slipped. I watched her little back-end sway away from me, her purse slung over her shoulder, and I thought to myself, *Have some respect for yourself, honey. You're the one going out with Nicholas Dunn.*

Thirty

I film Melody playing with her cats, drawing manga on the computer, doing some form of karate in the backyard, and climbing their huge oak tree. Mr. Butler told us that we should take as many film clips as we want. The video work has to be good, but the true art is in the editing. I keep this in mind as I try to capture monkey Melody flipping through the trees and yelling "AAAAAAAAAA" like Tarzan.

By seven p.m., it's dark and cold out, and I'm hungry. Melody is finally slowing down. The only time I actually saw her sit still was when she was doing her manga. Her artwork is really wild. She likes to draw evil-looking men with huge round heads, pointed features, and angled goatees. She's already sold her artwork to a few magazines and the covers of these magazines are framed in her bedroom.

While we're outside near the trees, her mother calls to us.

"Pizza is here," she shouts, and Melody leaps from the tree, running to the house.

"Come on," she yells. "Let's watch a movie. I'm exhausted."

I find this hard to believe, but follow her in.

I hate eating in front of people I don't know very well. They try to be sly, glancing at me now and then rather than full-out staring, but I know what they're doing. They're watching to see how much I'll consume. They want to see if I do weird things like cram whole pieces of cake into my mouth without chewing. I never eat like that. I don't even eat much more than other people.

Melody is on her fifth piece when I take a third.

We sit on the couch in the living room/dining room/ kitchen/family room area and Melody's mom comes to join us. She wears a long brown skirt that sweeps the ground and a matching brown turtleneck. She's thin and muscled, and she sways when she walks. I like watching her. It's like watching a willow tree in the wind.

"Did you eat any lunch today?" Melody's mom asks her.

Melody glances at me and then looks at her knees. She keeps her head down, picks at something on her pants, and glances at me again. I raise my eyebrows and look at her mother.

"Ritalin," her mother says. "She takes it in the morning, doesn't eat all day, and is starving by seven at night."

"Ah," I say and suddenly feel overwhelmingly

happy. She's flawed, just like me. No wonder I'm so comfortable around her.

"*Grease* okay?" asks Melody's mom and then she pops it into the DVD player without waiting for a response.

They don't look at me once while I'm eating my pizza. They sing along to the songs just like my family does, and Melody's mom tells us about the time she first saw *Grease*.

She was seven years old and went to see it with her older sister. She had only been to the movie theater one time before, and she felt like she'd gone to heaven. She still remembers the smell of popcorn, the sticky feel of the seats, the proximity of the big screen. It wasn't until the movie ended that she realized her sister wasn't sitting beside her anymore. She had crept back to the last row and was making out with some guy. Melody's mom, at the age of seven, stood and watched, getting her first lesson in French kissing.

I've never been to a movie theater. I've never seen a play. Dad won't go because he says the seats are uncomfortable; he'd much rather sit in his La-Z-Boy at home. He claims the seats are like whirlpools — they suck him in and won't let him out. Mom won't go because she doesn't want to leave Dad out. I won't go because if the seats are uncomfortable for Dad, they might be for me as well.

When "Hopelessly Devoted" comes on, Melody jumps up and grabs my hand.

"Come on, come on, come on," she says. "Pause the movie, Mom."

Melody pulls me down the hallway and into the room with the costumes. She rifles through the first row and pulls out a long white nightgown.

"Put it on," she says. "You have to sing this song."

"I'm not singing this song," I say. Melody shoves the nightgown at me and the light cottony material falls over my hands.

"You have to," she says. "You do it way better than Olivia Newton-John."

I look at her. Have I been singing "Hopelessly Devoted" in my film as literature II class? People must think I am completely psycho, a broken melon, a cracked cantaloupe. Melody is jumping up and down. I take the nightgown from her hand. I pull it over my head, and it fits. I stare down at myself. I am hardly Sandra Dee, but Melody does not seem to care. She has me by the hand again and is pulling me back toward the TV.

I follow.

If she's already heard me singing in class, why not sing for them now? Her mother heard me in the costume room; it's not like they don't already know.

Melody's mom hits play on the remote and "Hopelessly Devoted" begins. Melody keeps jumping up and down, even while seated on the couch. I don't know how she pulls this off, but she does. Her mother smiles at me, small creases fanning out from her eyes.

I open my mouth.

And I sing.

I walk around the room just like Sandra Dee, and I overpower her. I can barely hear the background music, but it feels so good to let it out. To feel like I don't have to be self-conscious.

When I'm done, both Melody and her mom stand up and applaud. I can't help it; I have tears in my eyes. I wipe them away on the sleeve of the nightgown.

"So," Melody says, still standing, her arms crossed over her chest, her pink hair shimmering before me. "How come you're not in concert choir?"

I shut my mouth. I feel my smile, my real smile, fading.

I shrug.

How do you tell someone who is utterly unselfconscious, who isn't embarrassed about anything except taking ADHD medication, that there is no way you can stand up in front of a teacher and audition? Stand up in front of someone who is probably thinking,

Where am I going to find a choir robe that will fit this girl, while trying to concentrate?

"Tryouts are in April," she says, her hands now on her hips. "I want you to try out."

She's nodding. Her voice is different. It's not demanding; it's soft, careful.

I shake my head. "I can't do it."

"You just sang in front of us," she replies. "You can sing in front of the choir teacher."

"You guys are different," I say, looking back and forth from Melody to her mom. "You guys are . . . comfortable."

Melody wraps her arms around herself.

"Hmm," she says.

We watch the rest of the movie. I still sing along, but I don't belt out the songs anymore. I've become self-conscious again, aware of my flaws. I wish I could be more like Melody — saying screw it to anyone or anything that might make me feel bad — but I can't do it.

I bike home slowly. Melody's mother offered to drive me, but I wanted to ride. I wanted to feel cool air on my face and to clean out my head. I like Melody. I like her house. I like her mom. I like having a friend I can be myself around. I hope she'll ask me to do something with her again, even if we are done filming her autobiography. I hope this one night isn't all there is to our friendship. I add Melody to my mental list of decent people in this world.

Thirty-one

The Spring Fling approaches fast. The decorations committee decides on a Spring-in-Spain theme, which makes about as much sense as summer in the Arctic, or Florida during a hurricane. Then I find out that Eva McGuire, girlfriend extraordinaire, has a sister at Oregon State University. Her sister was on some committee for something-or-other in the foreign language department and has access to decorations for a Spring-in-Spain dance theme. Eva seems cheaper and cheaper to me all the time.

Marcus Vemen, middle school bully from my youth, does pretty much all the work for our group. He prints the tickets, puts in ads for the dance through school announcements, finds out where we can hang posters, and figures out where to get the cash box. When he provides our group with all of the necessary information,

Melody says, "Good job," and Marcus Vemen grins like a three-year-old.

I think I might throw up. How can he be so happy when he's so awful? He doesn't deserve praise or happiness.

"I'll take care of the posters," Melody says. "Chelsea will take money at the front door."

I could reach out and kiss her when she says this. I look at her and give her a real smile, and she winks. Now I don't actually have to show up on the dance floor. If I sit at the front table, I'm excused to be a wallflower.

We are in our group, squashed into a lopsided circle with our desks, when I look down and see a perfect pair of feet. Trevor Laats stands between my desk and Melody's desk, allowing me the time to glance at his extremely nice-looking feet.

He coughs.

"Um, Mr. Butler says we're short two chaperones. Anyone have a parent who could show up to the dance?"

No one says anything.

Finally Bill, a gangly dark-haired junior who's shyer than I am, mutters.

"My mom will come if I ask her," he says, and then covers his mouth so we can't see his braces. His face flushes a deep red.

"Thanks, Bill," Trevor says. "My mom is coming too." Bill glances up quickly and the two of them nod together.

And then something very strange occurs. Someone I've never seen before and certainly don't know very well slips into my body and takes over. This person squeezes my voice box and forces me to speak.

"My mom will come if I ask her." Trevor looks at me and the two of us nod together.

"Thanks, Chelsea," Trevor says. "That's enough then. Just put their names down on this form."

I'm breathing so fast, I feel like I'm hyperventilating. When he says my name, it sounds like fine china, or maybe a clothing designer, a type of perfume, a supermodel, a famous shoe store. I take the form Trevor gives me, making sure my hand stays on the opposite side of the form from his, and write down Mom's name and phone number. I hand the form to Bill. When I give the form back to Trevor, I look up into his eyes. His glasses don't reflect light back at me like they usually do and for once they're not fogged up. I can see straight through the lenses and I stare into amber eyes that feel like sunsets and campfires.

He smiles at me and I smile back. No tight fake smile here, but a true grin that creases up into my eyes. I would offer up my mother for every dance until the end of time if it would mean looking into those eyes and feeling that smile. Trevor is beyond beautiful.

Thirty-two

I'm not sure how to tell my mom about the Spring Fling and her role. I know she'll embarrass me. No matter how she responds, I will be embarrassed by it. Either she'll think I've suddenly become infused with school spirit, or she'll think this is some bonding experience between the two of us that will turn us into lifelong pals. I would rather have asked my dad to come with me, but there's no way he would do it. Mom, on the other hand, will act like she won the lottery.

Rather than asking her, I leave the piece of paper on the kitchen counter — it is a copy of the one Trevor had me sign.

I know exactly the moment when she sees it. I'm sitting in the living room with my dad watching *Wheel of Fortune* on TV when all sounds from the kitchen stop. Mom had been extracting Marie Callender's frozen dinners from the freezer, unwrapping them, sliding them into the microwave oven, beeping the buttons, but all this stops and the silence that filters in from the kitchen is louder than the beeping.

I hold my breath.

I imagine her rushing into the living room, throwing her arms around me, and squashing up next to me on the couch. It gives me the shivers. I don't like my mom to touch me. I feel like every touch is a criticism, every hug has an ulterior motive: *Let's just see how big Chelsea is getting by trying to wrap my arms around her. Let's see how pudgy she feels when I put my arm around her waist and touch her rolls.*

But Mom doesn't rush into the living room and squash me. She doesn't run in and give me a big kiss on the cheek.

She starts singing. Singing. My mom never sings, but she's in the kitchen singing away to a song I don't recognize. Her humming is bad enough; her singing sounds like a squirrel trying to yodel.

As I listen, I relax my shoulders. I sigh, let out a small grunt, and think about how easy it is to make a parent happy.

Thirty-three

Melody decides that we need to pick out new jewelry for the Spring Fling to go with our new outfits. She has her costume all picked out, but she won't tell me what it is because she doesn't want to spoil the surprise.

"I want my outfit to be a surprise too," I say when she asks what I'll be wearing. I don't want to tell her that I haven't ordered anything and there's no way we're going shopping together.

I feel a moment of panic when I walk into Jesse's Jewelry on 39th because Eva is at the counter buying something and will probably make me feel like an ogre if she spots me.

Melody doesn't notice Eva, but does notice the fake-hair clips and makes a beeline for the display case.

I quickly follow and relax my shoulders when Eva walks out the door.

Melody is dressed like a cowhand today, in a straw hat and overalls. When she takes off the hat, she's got some pretty serious hat hair, but clips a green strand of polyester hair into her blond wavy hair anyway and then clips a strand of red into mine. She tilts her head to the side.

"Nope, hair clips aren't right on you." She plucks the clip out of my hair and sticks it in her own. Tomorrow she'll probably come to school as Rainbow Girl, or maybe Lady Gaga.

"I know what we need." Melody has found the friendship bracelets. They're woven in bright colors and she ties a purple, pink, and white one around my wrist. She ties a similar one around her own wrist. "Still not right," she says. She holds up a necklace, holds up some feather earrings, puts a tiara on my head, and then she stops. She grabs something so quickly that I don't see what it is, and before I can figure it out, she's at the counter paying.

I look at the jewelry where she had been standing, trying to determine what she's grabbed, but there are so many choices that I can't be sure of any of them.

When we get outside, she hands me a tiny paper bag. We sit on the bench outside the store, and she puts her hand on my wrist.

"We do this together, okay? Take off your right shoe."

"Right now?"

"Right now."

I'm wearing my black wedges with the leather straps, and I fumble with the buckle. I feel nervous, shaky, but I don't really know why. Is it because I'm doing a normal girl thing and I'm not always sure how to do that? Is it because I'm worried about what Melody has in her bag? What if I don't like it? What if I can't be honest about my smile and end up giving her a grimace when I should give her a grin?

I slip my shoe off and wait while she unlaces her farm boot and pulls off her sock. Her feet are pasty white underneath and kind of bony, but her toes are straight, her toenails trimmed.

"Now," she says.

We open the bags together and I shake a tiny ring into my hand. It's a toe ring. There's a small heart in the center of it with hands on either side of the heart. The ring has an open back so you can adjust it to fit on any size toe. I slip it on my second toe and stretch out my leg to admire it from a distance. My heart beats loud and strong in my chest; my smile is genuine.

"It's an Irish friendship ring. This means that we'll always be friends." Melody stretches out her leg too so our feet are together. The friendship toe rings shine, silver and pure, our toes the same even though her foot is pale, bony, and thin, while mine is olive-skinned and slightly rounded.

"Thank you," I say and glance at her. She's pink, all the way up to her ears, but she's smiling and glances at me quickly, then looks away again. "It's perfect."

"Just like our friendship," she whispers, but I hear her all the same.

Thirty-four

I finally order new clothes for the dance. Instead of jeans and a T-shirt, I'm going to wear a baby-doll tunic in deep purple over black pants. Two days later the box is waiting for me by the front door when I get home from school. I sneak it into my bedroom and pull out the clothes. I crush the purple shirt against my face and take a deep breath. Even though I'm tempted, I don't try the clothes on and won't let myself until the day of the dance. I'm worried they'll look terrible on me — turn me into a purple pumpkin, so I wait until the last minute. That way I can't change my mind and send them back.

On the night of the dance, I pull the clothes out of the box again. When I try on the shirt and pants, I feel chic and elegant. The tunic is snug in the proper places — right below my breasts and at the tops of my arms. My waist doesn't feel constricted, my thighs aren't being squeezed, and for once I don't feel like THE BLOB.

When I walk into the living room, Dad turns off

the TV and stands up. He takes my hand, bows, and kisses it.

I giggle.

Mom walks into the room and puts her hands on her hips. She looks me up and down and shakes her head.

"You look wonderful, Chelsea," she says. "Absolutely stunning. Just stunning."

I can feel my cheeks turning red, but it's nice attention. Maybe Trevor Laats will notice me and maybe Nicholas Dunn will drop dead.

Mom dresses up for the occasion as well. Rather than wearing her traditional tan and white, she digs out a red blouse from prehistoric times and puts it on over dark green pants. She looks like Christmas in March. My dad thinks she looks like the queen of England. He waltzes her around the room, bends her over backward, and gives her a big kiss.

She giggles. I wish she was always like this — happy, proud, noncritical. I could live with this mom.

Thirty-five

As we drive to the dance, Mom can't stop talking. She keeps telling me how my sophomore year in high school is shaping up as my best year ever. I've already made a friend. I'm going to a school dance. I might even become possible boyfriend fodder.

I stare down at my toes and wiggle them. My shoes are gold and silver Cinderella shoes. My purple toenail polish matches my shirt exactly, and the toe ring adds just the right amount of class.

"And before you know it, you'll be off to college. Have you given any thought to where you'd like to go?"

She looks at me. The lights from the dashboard glow red and orange, reflecting back at me from her eyes.

I shrug and look out the window. "Maybe I'll just go to community college and stay home with you guys," I say.

"Oh," she says. And nothing else.

Melody already has the table set up for ticket sales. She can only stay half the night. Her mom has a cast party for the Way-Off Broadway Theater, and Melody says she never misses a cast party, which involves good food, cute guys (although she says they're usually weird), and staying up really late.

"What do you think?" she says when Mom and I show up. She twirls around in a full-length formal dress that looks like Princess Kate should have been wearing it. It is pale pink and made of a shimmery, pearly fabric that clings to every curve of Melody's body. She would be beautiful if she hadn't decided to put her hair in a beehive. It stands up about a foot high so with Melody's stilettos, the hairdo, and her already tall frame, she looks a little bit like the Statue of Liberty.

Mom gazes up at her while I introduce them.

"Nice to meet you," Mom says, her smile showing all of her teeth. I can tell that she thinks Melody is way weirder than I am, which makes me feel pretty good about myself.

Mr. Butler is running around in circles. He's yelling things like, "Why isn't the microphone working?" "Turn the music down." "Where are my chaperones?"

He sees Mom, straightens his bow tie, flattens the tufts of hair that circle the lower part of his head, and then shakes her hand. He pumps it hard, salutes me, and ushers my mom into the gym, where the music is already thumping. I can hear him firing sentences at her while propelling her toward a dark corner of the gym.

"It's no big deal, really. Have you heard of something called freak dancing?"

"Freak dancing?" my mother says in response. She glances back at me and Melody before disappearing into the gym.

Melody and I look at each other, and then we both start laughing hard, so hard that I worry I'll break into a sweat. My mother is about to be initiated into the true essence of high school.

Melody and I sit down at the table and start selling tickets. A big cluster of kids gathers at the door, waiting for something to happen. No one wants to be the first one in the room, so they have to group together like lemmings and approach the table in a twitchy cluster. At first we don't have anything to do, and then we're mobbed.

So many smells float past me in a blur of jeans, high heels, skirts, and super-tight tees that I have to stop and sniff again when I get a full-blown boozy whiff of Grandpa Reece.

"Hey, Chubs," says a voice, and before I can stop myself, I look up — right into the blue eyes of Nicholas Dunn. Eva McGuire is attached to him in an overcoat sort of way, and they lean their full weight on the table. It scoots back and pushes against my stomach. Both Nicholas and Eva have lopsided grins and droopy eyelids. I imagine my Grandpa Reece hauling me over to the teeter-totter and balancing Nicholas and Eva on the other side.

"She is fat, isn't she?" Eva says. "I wonder where the hell she gets her clothes."

Eva flips her long hair over her shoulder by tossing her head and then dabs at the corners of her mouth with a black leather glove. It's spring, practically sixty degrees outside, yet Eva is completely wrapped in leather from head to toe. Even her hoop earrings are covered in black leather.

Melody is so busy selling tickets to a group of giggling freshmen that she doesn't notice.

"One ticket for Nicholas," Eva says loudly. "I don't have to pay because I'm in the class."

Nicholas Dunn hands me the five dollars while I pass him the ticket. His hand slides, hot and moist, over mine and I shiver. Nicholas Dunn stares at my chest. I glance down at myself, and I see my breasts straining at the cotton fabric. My shirt hadn't looked like this when I'd been standing up.

Our eyes meet and Nicholas opens his mouth, sticks out his tongue, and wags it at me. I get a good glimpse of the bloodshot whites of his eyes. I lean back in my chair and straighten my blouse.

"Nice melons, Chubs," Nicholas Dunn says, before

he and Eva zigzag away toward the gym.

"What did you say to her?" Eva says, but I don't hear the response because the door to the gym closes behind them.

My hands are sweaty so I wipe them on my pants. I look down into my lap and clutch my hands together, trying to stop their fluttering. I tug at the neckline of my shirt, but it stretches tight across my chest, revealing cleavage that I usually conceal with sweatshirts, T-shirts, and raincoats. Why did I think this shirt was a good idea? Why did I not cover my chest, knowing that an anthill of red bumps would appear there sometime during the night? Already it is starting and I hold my hand over my chest to cover both the cleavage and the bumps.

"They'll get kicked out," Melody says. Her line of freshmen has meandered, snakelike, to the gym door, and they're pushing one another forward and giggling loudly. Melody has to lean toward me and yell into my ear. "As soon as they start freak dancing your mother will have to make them leave."

I try to picture my mother kicking Nicholas Dunn out of the school and know that she is no match for him. He'd probably start grabbing his crotch and wagging his tongue at her while she clapped her hands together and shouted, "Shoo!"

The line has slowed down and most of the hesitant

pairs and groups have made their way into the gym. The doors are closed, but whenever someone comes out to get a stamp or to take a drink from the drinking fountain, we are blasted by flashing lights and thumping music. They're playing hip-hop and techno, mainly, and some retro stuff every now and then. I don't know any of the songs — I can't imagine them playing the theme song from *Oliver Twist*. I could probably dance to that.

"Gotta go," Melody says. Her mother has just walked through the door and is standing beside the table smiling down at us.

"Hello, Chelsea," Melody's mom says.

"Hello . . . Melody's mom," I say.

"Call me Jackie."

I feel a hand on my arm.

"Are you going to be okay?" Melody peers at me, her eyes meeting mine, holding them.

I shrug. The red rash across my chest has receded, and now that I've had a chance to sit here quietly, I feel okay. Grounded.

"Seriously. I think you'll be able to handle the line, but maybe you should have someone sit out here with you."

"I'm fine, Melody," I say. I kind of like the idea of sitting here by myself — avoiding the dark thumping, the skinny freshmen, the making out. I've only seen Trevor once all night, and when I saw him he was pushing a cart loaded with bottled water and individually packaged Rice Krispies treats into the gym. He wouldn't be able to sit with me, and I don't want Eva McGuire, Marcus Vemen, or anyone else to. Even sitting here with my mom doesn't sound very pleasant — I don't know what I would say to her in this setting. *So, freak dancing. What's up with that? Still want me to be boyfriend fodder? See why I hate it here?*

"Okay," Melody says, her voice low and slow. "But you be careful around those drunkards. I'll see you on Monday."

She does something that makes me blush and touch my face. She kisses me on the cheek — light and barely detectable, but I know it's there.

The two of them leave. It's a little after eleven, and the dance ends at midnight. I have forty-five minutes, so I start packing up the cash box, stuffing the extra tickets inside, counting the money, and arranging the bills. I watch groups of girls come hurtling out of the gym in clouds of moussed hair, high heels, and jeans. I watch couples sneak out of the gym, glance at each other with tiny, tight smiles on their faces, and leave through the main doors while holding hands. I watch groups of freshmen boys swagger through the entryway to the gym, hitting one another on the shoulders and pulling cigarettes from their pockets. I lock up the cash box, stand up to stretch my legs, and then walk outside to wake up a bit, get some fresh air.

It feels good outside, cool and damp. The air is fresh, untainted by sweat and aftershave lotion, so I take my time walking around the bike rack and between parked cars in the parking lot. I've never been at the school so late at night. It's eerily quiet, and feels like anticipation — as though something is about to happen, the calm before the storm. I catch glimpses of couples smashed up against the gym wall and as I make my way back to the gym, I can see cigarettes smoldering in The Achievement Gap.

I feel a hand on my arm.

"Chubby Chelsea," he says, twirling me around so I have to face him. His two buddies stand behind him, greasy grins on their faces and red-rimmed eyes roaming over me. I instinctively cover any possible bit of cleavage with my hand.

Nicholas circles around me, positioning himself between me and the doors to the gym. My back is to The Achievement Gap. His friends move in behind him, and the three of them back me up, right into the narrow opening between the gym and school. I glance behind me. The blank space of the alleyway seethes with threatening and mysterious shadows.

Nicholas steps toward me again.

"Chubby Chelsea. We need you to answer a question for us."

Nicholas stares at my chest. He drops his cigarette, crunches it with his heel, and takes another step forward. My heart thumps against my purple shirt, and I glance down at myself, wondering if he can see the movement under the fabric, if he can see the throbbing purple, a bruised aorta. My hand is not big enough. Bits of rounded skin peak out unwanted from beneath my fingers and my palm.

I have never been this far into The Achievement Gap. It seems like I could reach out and touch the bricks on both sides. Nicholas Dunn is so close, I can smell beyond the cigarette, beyond the alcohol, to the cheap cologne that makes my eyes water. One of his friends peers over his right shoulder, while the other looks over his left shoulder; with the light behind him, Nicholas and his buddies look like the shadow of the three-headed dog, Cerberus, who guards the gates to hell.

His hands reach out, and he smashes me against the brick wall of the gym.

"Brian . . . and I want to know," he says too close to my face, "what triple-D tits look like." One of the heads disappears from his shoulder as his friend moves to keep watch at the mouth of the alleyway. Nicholas's hands

113

press against my shoulders and my back rubs against the brick. My hand comes up to cover what remains visible of my breasts, but he grabs my arm, twists it behind me, and in one quick motion, yanks the elastic neckline of my shirt down so my breasts, still covered by my white bra, pop out of the top like bobbing apples. I look down at my exposed chest and listen to my breath. It comes in short bursts, fast and shallow. My head feels fuzzy, full, and confused. A sound goes off in my ears, a siren, a warning. I'm so surprised, so scared, that no sound comes out of me.

"What do we have here?" Nicholas says to his friend. "Two perfectly ripe cantaloupes. Chubby Chelsea, you could be a porn star."

Brian sniggers but never takes his eyes off of my bra.

Nicholas presses me against the brick wall, smashes my hands against the rough ridges behind my back, and then yanks the middle seam of my bra down hard. It tears and my breasts fall out, naked, pink, newly born. I turn my head away, squeeze my eyes closed. But even with my eyes shut, I see Nicholas Dunn's narrowed eyes and I can feel the wind trembling over skin that has never been exposed to an outdoor breeze before. This cannot be happening.

My breath comes faster and more shallow. I whisper, "Please stop. Let me go. Please don't." But I can't hear anything, and I'm not sure I've said it out loud.

I try to pull my hands out from behind me, hoping to free myself from the trap of my own body. I want to cover my chest, stop the show. When I open my eyes again, Nicholas Dunn is staring, as is his friend, and I can see the glint of their teeth against their bottom lips.

"No more, please. No more."

"Take the picture," Nicholas Dunn says. "Now!"

His friend pulls his phone out of his pocket and aims it at me. Nicholas Dunn is talking, but I only catch bits and pieces—"Get really close." "Don't get her shirt." "Post it later."

"Stop, stop," I say, but my voice comes out as an airy gasp.

"Hold her," Nicholas Dunn says, and Brian holds my arms against my back, wrenching my shoulders down.

"Daddy won't be happy when he sees how you flashed your titties at us . . . ," he says. "Brian let me . . ."

I see a couple of flashes and watch Brian's face light up for a second. He's holding an iPhone, newest version, black and sleek, with so many capabilities that I have no idea where the picture he took of me just went. Nicholas Dunn releases my arms, and with trembling hands I stretch my bra back over my breasts, but it won't hold together. I clutch at the broken bra, try to stretch it back over my chest, try to make it whole again, but the white fabric is now smudged with fingerprints, blackened and tainted, and I can't make the two broken ends unite. I snap the neckline of my purple shirt back into place and hold my hands over my chest. My rash is everywhere and all at once: my hands, my face, itchy under my hair. Nicholas and Brian look at the pictures on the phone and laugh. I don't want to see. I don't want to know. I take a step to the side, trying to creep past them, ready to run, but Nicholas, without even looking up, puts his foot against the wall and blocks my way.

"We're not done, Chubs." I hold my arms tightly against my chest, holding my body together, holding myself in, and try to slow my breathing. My heart pounds so loudly, it makes my head shake and my neck throb. Will this never end? How can time be moving so slowly? His fist lands in my stomach without warning and I double over, gasping, choking.

"Right here," Nicholas says, spinning me to the side. My head is pointed to the opening of The Achievement Gap and my butt is angled toward them. The flash of the phone camera goes off once, twice. I try to straighten, but my stomach is clenched and knotted so tight I can't release its hold on me. When I try, the muscles spasm and I throw up against the wall.

"Holy shit!" Brian says, flashing another picture of me. "Gross!"

The moments run together in my mind; I see Nicholas looking at the phone with Brian, I see Nicholas pull back his arm and punch me, I see Brian laughing, Nicholas laughing, the two of them laughing together — their teeth flashing in bits from the lights outside of the alleyway, and their mouths open in dark, black pits. My stomach muscles tighten and convulse, and I'm on my knees, looking down at trodden cigarette butts and gravel. I throw up again. My whole body shakes. I've lost any kind of control. I cannot survive this. I will not make it out of this alleyway.

Nicholas steps around me, straightens his shirt, straightens his jeans, and swipes his hands through his hair. It is then I hear a female voice over top of the other voices.

"Nicky. What were you doing in there? Who is that with you?"

Nicholas's buddies block the entryway to the alley with their bodies. Nicholas ambles over to them while pulling a smashed package of cigarettes from his back pocket. He shakes a couple into his hand. I want him gone, forever. If he would leave, I could breathe again.

"I just came out for a smoke," he says, and wrestles

his way past his bodyguards. "Let's get out of here. This dance sucks."

"Is that the fat girl?" Eva asks.

Nicholas grabs her arm and propels her away from the alley.

"There's nothing there, Eva," he says as they leave.

And I realize that's what I've become. Nothing.

When their footsteps fade and their voices are gone, I pull the side of my face away from the brick, put my back to the wall, and slide down. I sit on the wet ground, clutch my shirt and bra with my hands, trying to cover myself, trying to pull myself back together, but I'm shaking, trembling, and I'm cold.

I breathe.

My stomach clenches with tight, bursting pains and I throw up again. I can't stop. I lean over, away from the wall. I puke into the alleyway, and retch until my body feels weak and emptied. My breasts throb, my head feels raw, and my whole body is shaky. I feel drained and exhausted, beaten and exposed. I rest there until the shaking subsides and I feel like maybe I could stand up without toppling over. And as the trembling slows, my breath returns to normal and my eyes stop their leaking. I'm okay. I can walk. I can concentrate. I will be able to remove myself from this horrid place.

I move my gold and silver shoes out of the alleyway. I join a group of freshmen, and we make our way to the parking lot. Breath comes out of my nose in snorts. I'm pretty sure that some of those freshmen are staring at me, but for the first time in my life, I don't care. I hold my shirt in place, covering my torn bra, and force my legs to move in practiced motion. One step. Two steps.

I find my mom's SUV. I open the door, climb into the passenger side, pull my legs inside, shut the door behind me, and wait for her. I'm okay. I'm alive, but I have been exposed, humiliated, dissolved into nothingness, and I don't know where those pictures have gone. This might be it for me. I might never be able to function again.

Thirty-six

"Why didn't you come and get me? I've been looking all over for you. Remind me never to come to a school dance again. That was the most disgusting thing I have ever seen. Do you know what those kids were doing in there?" Mom looks wrinkled. I've only been in the car for about twenty minutes, but it feels like three hours. Her shirt is partially untucked from her green pants, and her crisply rolled hair is sticking out in tufts. She climbs into the driver's side of the car and talks.

I stare out the side window and clutch my shirt to my chest. Mom isn't looking at me. She's backing up and trying not to run over any kids or parents coming to pick up their kids.

"Do you even know what freak dancing is? Well, let me tell you, I got a first-hand lesson tonight. Those kids were having sex with clothes on. They were humping one another, doing things teenagers shouldn't even know about — that's what they call dancing. And my parents thought Nirvana was bad. I don't know what happened to decency, but your generation does not have it."

Mom's words blur. I stare at my reflection in the side window. My breasts throb. I tilt my head back against the seat and close my eyes. He'd called my breasts cantaloupes, luscious, delicious juicy fruits. Chelsea the porn star.

"Did you — " Mom begins, and I snap my eyes open.

I shake my head.

"Chelsea," says Mom, looking at me for the first time. "Is your face bleeding?"

I reach up to touch my cheek, and my hand comes away sticky. I put my fingers in my mouth and taste. Mom keeps looking at me, not paying attention to her driving, and suddenly slams on the brakes, narrowly missing the car in front of us, which has stopped for a red light. I don't even jump in my seat.

"Look at your hands, Chelsea," she says. "They're scraped raw."

I stare ahead and watch red change to green. Beyond the intersection, Mom pulls over to the side of the road and clicks on the dome light. She leans toward me, taking my chin in her hand.

"You have a huge scrape on your cheek and one on your forehead. Your fingers are all bloody. What in God's name happened?"

I look at her and blink. In fact, I almost laugh. How do you tell your mother that some guy from your accounting class exposed you — pulled down your purple shirt, the one that was meant to make you feel classy, and exposed not only your chest but the sore spot underneath? How do you tell your mom that you have been attacked? Assaulted? Put on exhibition like an animal?

"I just want to go home, Mom," I whisper. My teeth are clenched.

"And your clothes. What happened to your clothes? Your new shirt is torn and your pants are muddy. Did you fall? What is that stuff on your pants? Did you throw up?"

"I want to go home, Mom." My voice is slightly louder now. I lean back against the seat and turn my head away from her. I clutch my hands tight against my chest, willing my anger to turn inward, away from Mom, but her questions keep coming. I try to hum to myself, try to sing and whisper the anger out through my songs, but no lyrics fit this situation. I cannot stay here, in this place, a minute longer.

"Mom!" I shout. "Drive the damn car."

She jerks away from me and grips the steering wheel tightly with both hands, and she finally pulls back onto the road. We head home. She's no longer asking questions. I know that I've hurt her feelings, but I don't care. Hot tears drip out of the corners of my eyes.

When we get home, a pan of Dad's caramel brownies sits on the counter. I grab the entire pan and head to my room. I want to eat everything left in the pan while watching *Saturday Night Live*. I sit on the bed, my bra and purple shirt still clutched together with my right hand while my left hand grabs brownies and crams them into my mouth.

When I've eaten all the brownies, I get up, go to the bathroom, and throw up into the toilet. I lock the bathroom door behind me and pull my purple baby-doll shirt up over my head. My bra falls to the floor. I look at myself in the mirror, knowing that these size forty D breasts will soon be plastered over every social media outlet I've never signed up for. I'll be famous. I'll be tainted. I'll be damaged forever. My face scrunches up, ready to weep again, but I bite down on my lower lip until it throbs beneath my teeth. The rash is everywhere, across my stomach, up my arms, over my cheeks. Then I grab the purple shirt, which is resting on the counter, and rip it from the waist to the neckline. I tear right through the gathers that had enhanced my breasts, and I yank hard to rip through the elastic neckline. I look at myself in the bathroom mirror and gasp. How could this happen to me? What did I ever do to deserve this? I pant, wheeze, and sweat.

I go back to my room, pull on a sweatshirt, crawl under the blankets, pull them up to my chin, and watch TV all night. I don't want to think. I don't want to feel those hands on me, hear those words, smell that breath.

My anger slowly ekes out of me like drips from a leaky faucet, and around four in the morning I finally fall asleep.

Thirty-seven

I don't get out of bed all weekend. Dad comes into my room and sits on the bed, tries to coax me out with macadamia nut caramel popcorn, but I pull the covers over my head.

He's my dad. He can't know about what happened. What would he think if he knew those guys had seen my breasts? That right at this moment millions of online viewers could be laughing at his daughter's boobs and butt. I'm so sore, everywhere, but especially the small spot in the middle of my chest where my heart belonged and where little bits of hope resided. I had known who I was: Chelsea, the girl who would open a shoe store and present beautiful feet to the world. Now I'm not that girl. Why did this happen? Why me?

Mom comes into the room every half hour, trying to get me to talk to her.

"I know something happened, Chelsea. Won't you please talk to me? Tell me what happened? Did someone hurt you? Should I call Dr. Lawrence?"

I roll over and put my pillow over my head.

"She'll tell us when she's ready," Dad says, standing by Mom in the doorway.

I curl up into a ball. I want to cut off my breasts, slice them off, cut them into strips, and feed them to the neighbor girls. Didn't the Amazons cut off one of their breasts so they could fit their bow to their shoulders and chests without the breast interfering? I could become an Amazon and shoot Nicholas Dunn through one of his blue eyes, then cut out his heart, if he actually has one. Every time I think of Nicholas Dunn and his friends, I want to throw up all over again.

When Mom and Dad go to bed, I get up, go to the kitchen, and eat the rest of the macadamia nut caramel popcorn. I open the fridge and eat whatever I feel like. No fruits. No vegetables. No whole grains. Mom's Calorie Counters point chart is still posted on the fridge. I smear chocolate syrup over it.

Then I go back to bed.

Thirty-eight

Melody calls me on Saturday. She asks me how the ticket sales went. *Fine*, I say. She asks me if my mom had fun monitoring the freak dancing. *Yes*, I say. She asks if we made enough money to buy a new video camera for film as literature II. *I don't know*, I say. She spends about ten minutes telling me about the cast party and some guy who thought her hairdo made her look like Audrey Hepburn and how he'd always dreamed about meeting a girl who looked like Audrey Hepburn. She said he flirted with her all night long, leaning against her, putting his hand on her arm.

I thought about the hands pushing me against the wall, tearing through my clothes, taking pictures of my body. Nicholas Dunn was not flirting. He assaulted me, hurt me, broke me apart.

"Oh, and there's some really nasty pictures going around at school," Melody says. "Some girl's boobs were posted on like ten different people's Facebook pages. I'll send it to you."

"No," I whisper, but Melody isn't listening. She's forwarding the pictures, and I hear the swish of a received text. I push the phone against my ear, grip it tight in my hand, and will the picture to have been lost in transit, or to be so blurry and faded around the edges, I can't recognize the image.

"Some girls are just so skanky, you know? They should have some self-respect and not go around flashing every guy they see. I mean seriously, who is this girl anyway?" Melody says.

I don't respond.

Melody keeps talking. "Maybe you'll be able to tell who it is since you know who was at the dance."

I shake my head. I squeeze my eyes closed. I try to hold in the pain behind my nose and eyes, but tears leak down my face and drip from my chin. *I know who she is and she will dissolve, crumple into nothingness if those images appear on her phone.*

"I guess Principal Clark is pretty pissed off about the pictures," Melody says. "He's going to figure out who originally posted them, but that might be hard to do since they're all over the Internet and pretty much everyone at school has seen them."

I click the off button on the phone, drop it to the floor, and kick it under the bed. My laptop sits on my desk. I close it, unplug it, and slide it under my desk along with my purple shirt. Maybe if I don't see the pictures, I can pretend they exist in a different world, another dimension, somewhere over the rainbow where men are gentle and kind, speak in low, soft drawls, and protect women instead of humiliating them.

Thirty-nine

I become nocturnal. Mom comes into my room before work every morning and demands to know when I'm going to tell her what's going on — when I'm going to attend school again, but I ignore her. She can't make me go.

"Chelsea, I need to know. Were you raped?"

"No," I whisper.

She pats my foot under the blanket. I guess if I wasn't raped, then I'm okay.

At night, when Mom and Dad are asleep, I stare at myself in the bathroom mirror. I unhook my bra and try to imagine the picture that others are seeing, the picture of the skanky girl who flashed her boobs at Nicholas Dunn and his friend Brian. The scrape mark on my cheek turns into a scab, a scab like rug burn, and then slowly flakes away.

The mirror tells me nothing new, but when I stare, scrunch up my eyes, the image turns into a form without shape, a person with no edges.

I will never go back to accounting. I don't care what grade I get. I don't care if I fail the class and have to take it again next year. Nicholas Dunn is a senior; he'll be gone. At least he won't be in my class the second time around.

Melody calls every night, and every night I pull my blankets over my head when Mom comes into my room to tell me that Melody is on the phone.

I don't shower.

I don't wash my hair.

I don't paint my toenails.

I have had my body pulverized by a meat tenderizer. I am fat, dimpled, and that's what I'll have to show in my autobiography. Chelsea that skanky, dimpled chest-flasher with the cute little brown curls who doesn't need to do an autobiography because we all know everything about her already. How do you show that you've been broken apart when the image in the mirror still looks normal and whole?

Forty

On Friday, the day before spring break, I feel different; I feel like emerging. I don't know what's changed or why I feel slightly better, but I creep out of my blanket cave and sit on the couch. Dad's watching *Singin' in the Rain* and humming along.

When I sit down, he turns his La-Z-Boy so he can see me. I don't look at him. I stare at my feet.

"There's my little girl," he says. I know he means well, I know he loves me purely and truly, but I can't stop my bottom lip from shaking, or my eyes from becoming tight slits. I can't stop the fat drips that spill onto my sweatshirt. His little girl wouldn't have had size forty D breasts. That's a big girl.

I squeeze my eyes closed, trying to keep the tears from falling, but it doesn't work. My whole face scrunches up, crumples together, and a noise falls out of my mouth. It is a wail, a siren cry, a peacock shriek. The sound goes on and on.

Dad gets up from his chair and sits beside me on the couch. He puts his arm around my shoulders, but I shake him off. My dad. The safe one. I can't have him touching me, loving me, making me feel beautiful, because all that is tainted now. *Daddy won't be happy when he sees how you flashed your titties at us.*

I cry even harder. Dad places his hand on my back and rubs in a small circle. He hums along with Gene Kelly. I start to listen. His low song is nice, soothing. I let it enclose me, pull me in. I hiccup. Dad continues to rub and I lean into his hand. My breath stops coming in gasps and I rock back and forth. I watch Gene Kelly.

He can dance, he can sing, he's thin. My dad sings as well as Gene Kelly, but that's where the similarity ends.

Dad pulls his hand away from my back and I lean against the couch. We sit together and watch the entire movie. When it's over, Dad puts in *South Pacific*, and we watch that too. Mom comes into the room and sits on the other side of me. She doesn't try to touch me and neither does Dad. I'm wearing the same sweatshirt and pants I've worn for a week. When *South Pacific* is over we watch *The King and I*. At two o'clock in the morning, we all go to bed.

We watch movies, we hang out, but we don't talk, and I certainly don't sing. When I stand up from the couch, ready to watch more TV in my room, Mom stands up with me and puts her arm around my shoulders, tilts her head against mine, and stands beside me for a minute.

For the first time in a long time, I don't pull away.

Forty-one

On Saturday morning at ten o'clock, I'm out of bed, sitting at the table in the kitchen eating Dad's blueberry pancakes. He tops them with slices of strawberry, banana, and gobs of whipped cream. I'm thinking I might take a shower today — wash my hair. Maybe I'll even paint my toenails. It's spring break. I don't have to go anywhere — especially to school, especially to accounting.

And then the doorbell rings. I stop chewing and look out the kitchen window. Our kitchen window is right beside the driveway, but I can't see the front door from where I sit.

Dad, still wearing his cooking apron, wipes his hands on it and hums his way to the front door.

When I hear Melody's voice, and Dad's answering murmur, I examine the nooks in the kitchen, looking for a place to hide.

Dad leads Melody into the kitchen.

"I have been trying to get a hold of you ALL WEEK," Melody says, plopping down in the chair beside mine. Our table is round, making it harder for me to turn away from her. "Have you been sick?"

I finish chewing my mouthful of food and nod.

"Your mom told me where you live," she says, looking all around the kitchen. I follow her gaze to the cherry wood cabinets, tile floors, and stainless steel fridge. "Awesome."

Her cheeks are red, artificially rosy, and she's

wearing a little Heidi outfit with a short wide skirt, a white embroidered shirt, and green suspenders with red embroidery on them. Her hair is ribboned into two tight ponytails.

"You have got to tell me you're better," she says, looking at me again. She takes in my rumpled sweatshirt, greasy hair, and missing smile. "Are you?"

I raise my eyebrows. Am I? My breasts have been publicly plastered all over the Internet, and everyone at school has seen them without my permission. I am an object of ridicule. An outcast. Pariah. I have been assaulted and manhandled; I no longer know who I am.

I shrug.

"Good enough," she says, a grin pushing up her red cheeks, "because look what I have."

Melody holds up two strips of paper that she's clutching in her hand. They're a bit bent and damp, but she lays them on the table and flattens them.

"*Les Misérables*. Tonight. Mom got them for free and we are soooo going."

"I can't go," I whisper.

"Of course you can," she says, her grin not slipping.

My heart starts to thump in my neck. I instantly turn sweaty, feel a flush of heat racing across my chest, and know that I stink. She is so stupid. She just doesn't get it. She's cute, thin, uncaring, and full of energy. I stand up and walk to my room.

"Chelsea?" Dad says. "Baby?"

I pick up my pace, throw open the door to my room, and slam it behind me. I climb back in bed and pull the covers up over my head. I hear murmuring outside my door. Then the doorknob turns and someone comes in. The floor doesn't creak when this person enters. It's not my dad.

The bed barely squeaks when Melody sits. She doesn't say anything for a long time, and I know she's looking around my room, examining it. I don't have any manga on the walls. I have posters for musicals — *Oklahoma!*, *My Fair Lady*, *Singin' in the Rain*. Whenever the theater downtown puts on a musical, Mom asks them if I can have a poster. I swap in new ones every few months.

My room is clean. All week, Mom came in every day and carted out my empty dishes: plates, bowls, cups, glasses. All that's left of my mess is a heap of purple under my desk where I threw my shirt, my phone (which hasn't been charged in a week), and my laptop (which Mom puts on my desk every day and I put under my desk afterward).

"Listen," Melody says. "Your dad said that you came home from the dance with scrape marks on your head and torn clothes."

I don't answer.

I know they're all plotting against me. They're grouping in the hallway, whispering and murmuring, *Oh, poor Chubby Chelsea, someone must have called her fat.* Fat and chubby I can deal with; public humiliation and assault, I cannot.

Melody lies down beside me. "If you don't want to talk about it, that's cool with me. I gotta tell you, though, we NEED to go see *Les Mis*. It is so awesome. You know all the songs already, and I know you'll just love it. My mom did the costumes for all the characters, and they're wicked —"

I throw back the covers and sit up in bed. One minute I want to bawl; the next minute I'm pissed as hell. I look at Melody. She's still lying down but her eyes open when I sit up.

"Don't you get it?" I say in a low voice. "Don't you understand? Look at me. I'm fat. I'm huge. I'm disgusting. I probably won't even fit into the theater seats, just like my dad. Don't you get why I've never been before? They don't make theater seats for chunky girls. They make theater seats for skinny beautiful people who don't get tormented and bullied."

I'm breathing hard, snorting through my nose, and I glare at Melody. I cross my arms over my chest and say, "Get the hell out of my room and leave me alone."

I'm pretty sure she will run away and never want to see me again.

Melody sits up slowly and meets my glare. Her grin is gone and her eyebrows are down. Way down.

"Now you listen here," she says, her hands balled into fists. "I don't know where this bullshit is coming from, but I'll tell you right now, you will fit into those seats. In fact, those seats were made for you — you, especially — someone who loves music and will enjoy every minute of it. And if you don't go with me, I will be pissed as hell. Look what I brought."

Melody shrugs out of the small earth-green sack that had been slung like a backpack over her shoulders. Out of it she pulls a silk shawl. It's purple, gold, and black, and shimmers like something alive. She lays it across the tops of my hands, which are clenched around my comforter. I turn my hands over and feel soft sweetness. And just like that, the anger oozes out of me.

"It will match that purple shirt perfectly. Which, by the way, looked gorgeous on you."

Without thinking, I look at my desk, at the purple mound curled under it. I clutch the silk shawl and bring it up to my face. I breathe it in and when I pull it down again, my tears shimmer on its glossy surface.

"I tore that purple shirt," I whisper.

"Is that it?" Melody asks and points to my desk.

I nod.

"Ha!" she shouts. She jumps off the bed and picks up the purple shirt. "My mother can fix this in two seconds, if you want her to."

I try to wipe my tears off of the shawl with my fingertips. I glance at the shirt, then back at the shawl. Could I wear the shirt again? Maybe the shawl could make it like new, fix the taint that was Nicholas Dunn. It might be okay. Melody pauses and then sits down beside me on the bed.

"Chelsea, something bad happened at the dance," she says, reaching out and touching my cheek with her fingertips. "And if you don't want to see *Les Misérables* with me, I'll accept your decision. But I really want you to go. I really want to see this musical with you because you know the story. You will love every minute of it. I don't want to go with anyone else but you."

"Why?" I ask, and sniff.

"Why what?" she says.

"Why me? Why are you so nice to me?"

"Shit," she says. "You can't figure that out?"

I glance at her. She's shaking her head and biting her bottom lip.

"Chelsea," she says. "Look at me. I can't slow down. I drive everyone crazy. My friendships only last a few weeks. Guys are totally freaked out by me. I need you. You're good for me. You're patient, quiet, mellow. I like being around you. When I'm with you, I feel grounded."

She sniffs. She rubs her sleeve under her nose. She blinks hard.

I lift my arm, my heavy arm, and drape it over her shoulders. She leans against me, her head on my shoulder, and we sit sniffing for a couple of minutes.

When she pulls her head away, we both look down.

"So will you come?" she asks with a wobble in her voice.

At that moment, I love her. She needs me. I've never been needed in my entire life. It feels really, really good.

"Yeah, I'll come," I say, and try to smile, but I don't feel very happy.

Melody sniffs, shakes her head, and wipes her eyes. She nods once.

"We'll pick you up at six-thirty. I'll have the shirt ready."

We glance at each other and then look away. We smile small, tight smiles, and then she leans over and kisses me on the cheek.

"You're like a campfire," Melody says to me, and then darts out of the room. I hear the front door slam and then lay back on the bed.

I think about Nicholas Dunn smashing me against the brick wall, taking my picture, tearing my bra, and exposing my breasts, and I wonder how two people can make me feel so differently about myself.

I have about seven hours to get ready for my first ever live musical. Nicholas Dunn won't be there, and if I see anyone from school, I'll pretend that the boobs in the pictures weren't mine, and I can't believe that anyone would do such a thing, or have such a thing done to them.

Forty-two

The musical is amazing. It is so much better than watching the movie; I can't believe I've been satisfied with two dimensions. Seeing *Les Mis* live makes me tingle from my fingertips to the roots of my hair, and I want to be up there on that stage like nothing I've ever wanted before. I want to be Cosette, belting out the songs and feeling the music rip through me. I can barely breathe.

Mom and Dad are sitting in the living room watching

Casablanca when I get home, but they turn the TV off and swivel in their chairs to listen to me rave. Both of them smile as I twirl around the room, talk with my hands, and bounce on the couch.

Melody's mom fixed my purple shirt. She added a strip of black material right down the middle. The black material has gold buttons on it. The shawl matched the shirt so well, I can't imagine ever wearing one without the other.

"You guys have to come with me and see *Les Mis*. Dad, you will totally fit in the seat," I say, turning to him and putting my hand on his arm. "I didn't even think about it while I was there. Come on, come with me."

"Oh, Chelsea," Dad says, pulling on his beard and turning his head away. "I'm happy sitting at home in my chair. I work all day, and when I get home I like to relax in a comfortable environment. I find my chair comfortable. But if you enjoyed it so much, you need to go again. Often. Whenever you want. It's so good to see you happy."

I lean back on the couch and throw my arms wide.

Mom gets up from the other chair and comes to sit beside me. She takes one of my hands in hers and holds it, just holds it.

"Chelsea," she says, "are you going to tell us what happened at the dance?"

I sigh and say, "Someday, Mom, someday. Okay?" In my head I'm thinking I will never ever tell her what happened. How do you explain the most embarrassing moment of your life to your parents? How do you show them your most vulnerable moment when you were helpless and humiliated? They don't even know about the song the neighbor girls sing to me.

I slip my feet out of my gold and silver shoes and wiggle my toes. I'd painted my toenails purple again, to match my shirt and shawl. I'd even put black and gold stars on them and, of course, I'd worn the friendship toe ring.

Mom stretches out her feet beside mine and we compare. Her feet look skeletal next to mine — bony and knobby.

"Chelsea," she says, "your feet say so much about you. I guess feet can be the windows into our souls, can't they?" She laughs.

And that's when it hits me. That's when I realize what I want to do for my film as literature II autobiography. My feet are who I am. They represent Chelsea.

Forty-three

Melody and I hang out almost every day during spring break. I can see her starting to drive my mom crazy. She's everywhere at once. She's in the kitchen, in the living room, in my bedroom, in the bathroom, in my parent's bedroom. I don't know what she was doing in my parent's bedroom — probably digging through my mom's closet to find some retro nineties clothes — but after Mom caught her in there she scooted her out and reorganized the closet.

Melody made my dad laugh so hard, I thought he was going to have a heart attack. She insisted that he arm wrestle with her. They crouched across from each other over the coffee table in the living room and went at it. Melody stood up, used her entire body, both hands and all her weight, but she still couldn't budge my dad's arm. He laughed himself red in the face.

And for a few days, I smiled again.

As the end of spring break approached, I stopped smiling. I knew I needed to go back to school, but I felt queasy every time I thought about Nicholas Dunn and sitting behind him in accounting. Even the thought of it made the rash across my arms and chest flare up and settle into bumps. I couldn't hide forever, but I sure as hell wanted to.

Forty-four

On Thursday night, I meet Melody at her house. She says she has something *awesome* to show me, which probably means her mom made a new costume that will turn Melody into Oprah. I ride my bike over to her place and lean it against the door to their garage. I sniff the air. It smells like wet soil, earthy and musky. It's a good smell, fresh and clean. Who would have thought earth can smell clean?

Melody meets me at the door and I follow her into the house.

"We have to wait until it's dark," she says.

We mess around on her computer for a while. She pulls up her Facebook page and shows me all of her manga posts, and photos of herself wearing various costumes. She has about nine hundred online-only friends who message her constantly; she says she almost always stays up past midnight just responding to posts.

She says some guy in Japan wants to marry her and then the two of them will do manga together for the rest of their lives.

She shows me a picture of the guy from Japan. His hair is pink and spiked straight up. In his picture he's leaning against a brick wall, which is completely covered with a spray painted cartoon woman in a skintight leather outfit. Her boobs don't look like they're in proportion with the rest of her body — kind of like Barbie. If this cartoon woman were alive, she'd probably be unable to walk upright because her breasts would tip her forward. I wonder if Nicholas Dunn would smash her against a wall to expose her thirty-two triple-D boobs.

I look at Melody out of the corner of my eye. She's admiring the manga character on the wall.

"You're not going to fly over there and visit him, are you?" I ask.

"Huh? No way," she says. "I may be hyper, but I'm not stupid. He's probably a pedophile."

I look at the guy's picture again. If he's a pedophile, he's a pretty young one. But he definitely looks a little weird — but then again, I wouldn't consider Melody the epitome of normal.

Melody looks at her screen and makes a couple clicks.

"These are the pictures that everyone at school has

been talking about, the ones I sent you," she says. "Did you look at them?"

Before I have a chance to cover my eyes or run to the bathroom, before I can explain that I deleted her texts without looking at the pictures, Melody clicks on a somewhat blurry and dark photo that, when enlarged, turns out to be a pair of D-sized breasts. They can't possibly be mine. My boobs are not round, light pink, with perky nipples, and they certainly wouldn't consume the entire screen with no room for a purple shirt, any sort of background, or a hint of who might be behind those breasts.

"Kind of crazy, huh," she says.

I thought it would be more obscene. When I remember that night, there was pulling, pushing, crippling fear, and hot embarrassment. There was force and blood. These are just a couple of breasts that look like they could use some sunshine.

"I wish mine looked like that. I mean, honestly, it's not fair." Melody pulls her black ninja shirt tight against her chest and reveals small mounds that compare to my mounds back in third grade. "I'm so flat I look like a boy. It would be nice to have, you know, a handful, or something." She puts her hands over her chest and that pretty much covers them up. "If I had boobs like this chick, I'd plaster them on the Internet too."

"No, you wouldn't," I say.

"Well, okay. Maybe not. Still, they're pretty nice."

"But maybe she didn't want that picture taken, or maybe she didn't know it would be taken and would end up on Instagram."

"Yeah, that would suck. If someone did that to me, I'd get them back so fast. I had someone copy one of my manga pictures and use it on their website. I was so pissed. I sent warnings to all the manga artists I know, to tell them not to trust the site. They're totally exposed now and no one I know buys their stuff." Melody looks at the picture again and nods slowly. "But if this girl wants to be a porn star, she's already viral."

Like a bad virus. One that can't be cured.

When it gets dark, Melody leads me into her backyard. There is a sliding glass door through their living room/dining room/kitchen/family room area that leads to a back patio. Right now, the back patio is bare except for two clay pots and two camping chairs. Melody sits in one, I sit in the other.

Melody is grinning like crazy. She keeps letting out these high-pitched peeps and then grabbing the material of her skirt.

"Wait," she says quietly, holding up her hand.

I wait. I wait a long time.

It's warm, surprisingly warm. I'm pretty sure the temperature is in the sixties, which feels kind of nice as I sit looking around me. It's quiet and dark in her backyard. Her house backs up to a creek, a ravine filled with trees and bushes. There are no streetlights behind her house, just a soft glow reflected off the clouds. It smells like camping. The best thing about sitting in Melody's backyard with her is that we don't talk, and the silence isn't uncomfortable — it actually feels good.

As I'm sitting there, starting to feel my eyelids droop and my muscles relax, I see a shape about fifty feet in front of us. It's so dark that I can't make out what it is. Melody's hand touches my arm and she sits forward. I lean forward too.

The shape becomes a little bigger, a bit clearer. It's fairly large, with four legs and a sleek body.

It's a deer. Right in her backyard.

And that deer is followed by two miniature deer with flashes of white on their backs. I realize then that I'm not breathing.

The deer lean forward on their delicate legs, their long necks stretched forward. Neither Melody nor I moves. And as we sit, perfectly still, the deer creep closer. When they're about ten feet away from the clay pots, a little one shoots in front of her mother. The baby sticks her nose right into the pot and comes up munching. The fawn's ears are huge — far too large for its narrow, angular face. The mother sticks her face into the other pot as does the other baby.

I'm sitting about ten feet away from them. Their eyes, so deep and black, glance at us, glance away.

I'm scared to move. The muscle in my lower back starts to ache from my leaning forward, but I worry that if I sit back, the deer will run.

Even their chewing is careful, delicate. I hear the crunching of nuts or seeds between their teeth, but their mouths stay closed and their eyes soak up the darkness around them. They nuzzle their way to the bottom of the pots, and then turn around and step through the grass to the bushes by the river.

Melody and I look at each other.

Melody whispers to me, "When I sit here and watch them, I understand what beautiful is."

Beautiful is sitting with a friend, feeling at peace with the world, and not having to worry about rashes, exposed breasts, and a tormentor named Nicholas Dunn.

Forty-five

I can't sleep Sunday evening. All night long I imagine Nicholas Dunn with his shaggy hair flying as he grabs at me, laughs at me, and pushes me against the brick wall. I fall asleep for minutes at a time and then jerk awake thinking about him. I shiver, sweat, and feel sick. I watch the light in my room change from black to gray. The morning's tentacles of the sun reach to me across the bed and make me clutch at the comforter.

Skipping school again sounds wonderful, but I have to go. I'm falling way behind in my classes. I wash my hair, scrub my body, and let the hot shower water pour over my head. I wish the world didn't have assholes in it. But it does. And sometimes they're not just assholes, but miserable tormenting assholes.

I dress carefully — choosing comfortable jeans, a matching heather-gray cardigan and shirt set, and black shoes with open toes and open heels. It's raining, hard, so I wrap my yellow slicker around me and walk to the garage. I swallow the bubbles erupting from my stomach and concentrate on getting to my bike. I've taken too long and find myself walking down the path from our front door alongside the neighbor girls, who are wearing matching purple slickers covered in pink kittens. We peek at one another from beneath the hoods of our raincoats, and they start their chant.

"Fatty, fatty, two-by-four. Couldn't fit through the bathroom door. So she did it on the floor. Fatty, fatty, two-by-four."

They climb into their SUV, and I walk around the house to the garage. I open the side door and grab my bike. I wheel it to the driveway, hop on, and head down the street. As I pass the SUV, Carla, the mother of the three girls, is strapping them into their booster seats. They are still chanting.

Forty-six

I slink into my assigned seat in Spanish and my teacher, Señorita Spazarna, whose real name is Ms. Sparna, rushes over with three pounds of worksheets that constitute my makeup work. For once in my life I am thankful for makeup work; I start filling in the blanks and keep my eyes focused on my work so I don't have to look at anyone.

About twenty minutes into the class period, right when Señorita Spazarna is demonstrating the action *para saltar* by leaping off the table in the front of the room and landing on both feet with her hands out, the intercom beeps and Principal Clark's voice invades the class.

"As many of you know," he begins, and I immediately wonder if we've been bombed by China, "some misbehavior occurred at the Spring Fling dance. Today we will be holding a special assembly in the gym to discuss this misbehavior and the attention it received these last few weeks through social media. Please follow your teachers to assigned areas in the gym and remain seated with your class. The assembly should be concluded in about twenty minutes."

Señorita Spazarna claps her hands and shouts quick, crisp orders in Spanish that none of us understand, and then marches to the door where she flicks the lights on and off. I carefully, slowly fill my backpack, sliding in my extra makeup work, trying not to crumple the packets while my hands shake uncontrollably and my arms break out into that bumpy, red rash. I know what this is about.

The class noisily ambles down the hallway and I make my way to the back of the group. I pull the sleeves of my cardigan down over my arms, trying to conceal the flaming rash that is starting to itch, but the sweater has three-quarter sleeves, and my wrists and hands are still visible, angry with bumps.

We file into the gym and I climb up the bleachers with the rest of my class and sit in the fifth row. Other classes quickly fill in the remaining seats, and soon the gym is packed beyond capacity. I consider pulling a fire alarm but don't see one handy.

The girl next to me squirms and slides over, and Melody appears and sits beside me. I almost wrap my arms around her. She has no idea why this moment terrifies me, but just her presence makes me feel better.

"This will be a joke," she says.

I am unable to speak. I can't think of any joke that I could possibly laugh at in this moment, in this place.

Principal Clark stands at a podium in the middle of the gym and taps on the microphone. Crackling static overpowers the noise in the room and we gradually quiet. He looks out at us, not speaking for a time, and finally clears his throat.

"It has come to our attention that some disturbing behavior occurred at the Spring Fling dance. Many of you have seen the images posted on Facebook or through Instagram or other social media outlets, and we would like to address the issues brought up by these images. First, I want to say this."

He looks out over the audience and tries to meet the eyes of as many students as he can, but there are about two thousand of us, and pinpointing that many just isn't possible. I can't sit still, and again yank at the sleeves of my sweater, trying to cover my hands.

"If you took the pictures, if you are in the pictures, if you in any way know who is responsible for these images, we would like you to come forward. We would like to get to the bottom of this. Secondly, this is an issue of respecting oneself and respecting others. That is why we have brought in a speaker today who will be addressing . . ."

I don't hear the rest of Principal Clark's message. *If you took the pictures, if you are in the pictures, if you in any way know who is responsible for these images, we would like you to come forward.* The ringing in my ears is so loud, the thumping of my heart so painful, that I clutch my chest. I rock back and forth on the bench and feel Melody's hand on my arm. I have to leave. I have to leave now.

I stand up, struggle through the people in front of me, and make my way down the five steps of bleachers. I stumble past the first row and push open the doors to the gym. I lean my head against the wall in the hallway and try to blink back the darkness that pushes at the edges of my vision. I feel a hand on my back and hear a voice beside me.

"Deep breaths. Deep breaths," Melody says.

I try to slow my breathing, try to follow the advice

of the person behind me, but I have just been called out in front of the entire student body. I have been told that I don't have self-respect, that I don't care about myself. I am the one at fault, it seems, and that's how the whole school sees me — even if they don't know it's me. What am I supposed to do? What can I do? I drop to my knees in the hallway and hear some scurrying behind me. Arms appear on either side of mine, pulling me up, lifting me to my feet, helping me down the hallway. The door to the nurse's office opens and I am guided to the bed at the far end of the room. The light is so bright in here, so flashing and revealing, I close my eyes. I want to faint, pass out, close my eyes and forever forget, but the blackness at the edge of my vision begins to recede, and soon the pounding in my head quiets and my breathing slows. I put my hand on my forehead and open my eyes.

Melody and the school nurse both peer down at me. Melody's eyes are huge in her face and her pupils are dilated. Maybe mine look the same way. The nurse smiles at me and I notice then that she is holding my hand. Squeezing it.

"Ah, good," she says. "You're coming back around."

"Geez, Chelsea. I thought you were dying."

The nurse laughs a nice, calm chuckle and squeezes my hand again.

"Now, now, we never thought that, but we wondered

if you might faint. It looks like we're out of that danger. Would you like some water?"

I nod and she disappears from my vision. Melody moves closer and stares down at me. Her breathing is coming faster than mine.

"You scared the shit out of me," she says. "I am not good in emergencies, okay? Don't do that."

I close my eyes and listen to my breathing. Slow and steady. Calm and relaxed. *If you in any way know who is responsible for these images, we would like you to come forward.* I cannot live this way. I cannot deal with this bullshit. I never want to see any of these people again.

Forty-seven

Mom arrives about an hour later and I can tell she's frustrated. I get it, I guess. I skipped the whole week before spring break, I stayed home during most of spring break, and my first day back at school lasts about half an hour before she's called in to bail me out. She hunkers down with the nurse at the door and the two of them whisper back and forth. I catch only words and phrases — *anxiety attack, red rash, hyperventilating.*

Mom nods a lot and I watch her narrowed eyes widen and her frown relax. Maybe I'm not faking after all.

In the car on the way to Dr. Lawrence's office she asks me if I'm feeling okay now, if I thought I was going to faint, if something had triggered this reaction. I lean my head against the cool glass of the car window and watch the rain drip into puddles at the side of the road, land with a soft *plip* that sends a funnel of water up with a splash. I don't know if I will ever feel right again.

I sit on the table in Dr. Lawrence's office and swing my feet back and forth. Mom is attempting to answer the questions Dr. Lawrence is asking her, but she doesn't know the answers and I'm having a hard time hearing the questions. Dr. Lawrence takes my face in her hands and looks at my cheeks, at my neck, at my arms. She asks me if I have the rash on my stomach. I ignore her. The door to the examination room opens and shuts and I am alone with Dr. Lawrence. She rolls her chair next to the examination table and waits. I take a quick look at her to see if she is watching me. She is. I swing my legs harder and faster.

"Chelsea, I'd like you to look at me."

I turn my head and try to focus on her, but it's so bright in the room, I have to squint my eyes, which makes Dr. Lawrence's long face even longer. I would laugh but I feel too flustered and confused.

"Can you tell me what happened?"

She crosses her legs and waits patiently. I clear my throat and think about the issue, the issue of respecting oneself. The issue of having self-respect, or the lack thereof. No self-respecting young woman would allow pictures to be taken of her breasts and posted online. A self-respecting young woman would come forward. A self-respecting woman would have been able to fight back, to ward off the attack.

"I almost fainted," I say.

"Did something happen? Did you feel sick?"

"There were so many people in the gym, I had to leave."

Dr. Lawrence stands up beside me. She leans against the table and crosses her arms over her chest. She has no boobs. Flat as a pancake. No triple-D there.

"You have hives. All over your body. You are having an extreme reaction to . . . something. It's my guess, although I'm not sure since I'm missing some pieces of the puzzle, that you had an anxiety attack. Your mom claims that you get these bumps quite often," she says. "Is that correct?"

I hold my arm up and look at the rash. It's the same one; it's nothing new. Hives. Huh. I thought you got those from poison ivy or cat allergies. I get them from Nicholas Dunn and all-school assemblies.

"I believe what we're looking at here is a social anxiety disorder. Do you know what that is?"

The gray carpet under the examination table has a big orange splotch on it in the shape of an igloo. An orange igloo. Like a melon. Cantaloupes.

"It means that you have a reaction, a rather severe reaction in situations involving many people. Your mother said that you had hives when you attended the Calorie Counters meetings and that you often develop hives during extended family events. Does that sound right?"

I'd like to see Dr. Lawrence at a family event with Grandpa Reece. I wonder if Dr. Lawrence likes musicals. She probably thinks musicals are pedestrian and corny, and she probably only attends the symphony or opera or lectures on the bird flu and outbreaks of meningitis.

"I'd like you to try something for me. I'd like you to take a very low dose of a drug called Maxin. I want to see if the hives go away when you are on this drug. Usually we would have you psychologically evaluated first, but your hives are covering your entire body, so we need to treat this immediately. I have a trial dose for teens. You'll take it for three days and we'll see if you can manage school and attend classes. It will feel a bit disorienting at first, but the effects should even out after you take it for a few days. Does that sound okay to you?"

I am unable to attend school, Dr. Lawrence. School may very well kill me. Dr. Lawrence puts her hand on my arm and leans close. She smells like baby powder. I tilt my head away and close my eyes. I just want to go home, go away, disappear into myself. Just give me the pills and let me go.

"There's nothing to be ashamed of, Chelsea. Many people suffer from social anxiety disorders; it is an extremely common problem. Let's see if we can't figure it out and take care of these hives."

I just want to be left alone. By everyone. I want to curl up in my bed, pull the covers over my head, and count the spots that appear at the back of my eyelids.

In the car on the way home, Mom tells me how much she dislikes the idea of teenagers taking medication. How doctors hand out prescriptions like candy and complicate the issues, causing side effects that are worse than the original problem.

I can't imagine any problem worse than Nicholas Dunn, breasts exposed on the Internet, and the notion that it's all my fault.

Forty-eight

My mom and dad whisper about me a lot. Dad sits in his La-Z-Boy, the footrest up, the backrest down, and clicks through the channels on the TV. Mom crouches next to his chair and whispers at him, frantic, with lots of P's and B's that catch air. When I sit on the couch, she gets off her knees and says something loud, like, "and that's why Sylvia really needs to find another job." But I know that Sylvia was not the main topic of conversation, not until I came into the room.

This used to happen a lot in elementary school PE — the whispering, the changing of the topic when I walked into the room. Changing for PE was no big deal in first grade and second grade, when the girls and boys pretty much had the same body shapes, but when third grade came along, everything shifted. I started to get breasts already but had no clue what a bra was. My mom, size thirty-six B, could get away without wearing a bra pretty much all the time, under any type of clothing, in all circumstances including work meetings and large group presentations. I didn't think wearing a bra was a big deal either, so I didn't wear one. I mean, really, what nine-year-old needs a bra?

One day in third grade, I'm changing for PE beside

Lindsay and Ashley. Both of them have their hands up and are covering their mouths. I know they're whispering and I'm pretty sure they're whispering about me, since they keep looking at me. But I have no clue what they're saying and don't really care. They whisper a lot.

When we run our laps around the gym, Lindsay and Ashley include a couple of other girls in on their secret, and all four of them are whispering behind their hands and watching me jog around the gym. I look down at myself, at my crisp white T-shirt that my mother has ironed, at my navy-and-white gym shorts that I've tucked my T-shirt into, and at my shoes. Laces are tied, my butt is covered, my T-shirt is clean, and I don't smell. What are they staring at?

After PE, I'm in front of my locker, getting ready to change out of my gym clothes, when I hear a cough behind me. I turn around and the three girls stand in a semicircle with me as the flat end. Ashley speaks first.

"My brother told me that they're called hooters," she says. "If you have more than a mound you need a bra."

I look down at my chest. Mounds. Like the ones in our backyard where the mole dug up our flower beds.

Ashley pulls her T-shirt tight against her front and looks down at her incredibly, inexplicably flat chest — absolutely no mounds whatsoever, but the outline of a training bra.

"See? I have boobs so I'm wearing a bra. You should too. It's not right to be running around the gym without a bra when your hooters are flopping around. We think you should wear a bra." The three girls beside her examine my chest, examine the mounds that push against my T-shirt, and all of them surreptitiously glance down at themselves to check out their own hooters and then at each other. They're all wearing bras. They're all flatter than I am.

That night I tell my mom I need a bra. We go to the store and Mom brings four different training bras into the dressing room with us. She twists them this way and that, trying to make them cover my hooters, but already my mounds peak out the edges of the cups and make the bras look like too-small triangles taped to my chest. She goes back out to the intimates section of the store and comes back with four more bras, all cup size A. I skip the trainers and go right for the full-on bras. I buy the ones with the blue cloth flower right between the cups.

Forty-nine

At seven o'clock the next morning, Mom shows up at the side of my bed with a glass of water in one hand

and a pill in the other. For someone who doesn't believe doctors should be handing out pills like candy, she's pretty eager for me to consume narcotics before I've even had breakfast.

"Dr. Lawrence said that you need to take this at least an hour before you would encounter a social situation. School starts at eight-thirty, so let's have you take this now."

She sits at the side of the bed and hands me the pill. It is yellow with the word Maxin on one side, and the number 10 on the other. It is then that I realize what I'm about to do. I agreed to this to escape from Dr. Lawrence, but do I really want to be drugged so I can get through the day? How will I survive the day without being drugged? I've never taken anything stronger than Advil. What will Maxin do to me?

I put it on my tongue and consider sliding it underneath so I don't really take it, but I remember that I have accounting today. Nicholas Dunn will be contaminating the very air in the room with his poisonous presence and only a yellow pill will dilute the pollution. I remember that I only have three pills; this is a trial run. If I don't like them, if they don't work, I won't take any more. I swallow the pill and take a swig of the water in the glass Mom holds. She stands up, smooths the nonexistent creases out of her pants, and smiles down at me. She takes the glass from my hand and backs out the

163

door, watching me as she goes. I wonder what she sees.

Nothing happens.

I take a shower, blow-dry my hair, brush my teeth, eat some breakfast, and I still don't notice anything. It's when I head outside to get my bike that I realize something might be a little different. The neighbor girls are outside, climbing into the family SUV, and usually I would wait inside, peak out the side window by the door, and hold my breath until they drove away, but today I see them walking the fine edge of the curb, and I go outside anyway. All three girls turn to look at me, and their mouths open at almost exactly the same time. So does mine.

"Fatty, fatty, two-by-four. Couldn't fit through the bathroom door. So she did it on the floor. Fatty, fatty, two-by-four."

The doctor said it could be disorienting, and disorienting is exactly how it feels. I am outside of myself, looking in, and don't really care who sees me or what they think of me. Strangely, I find myself walking toward the girls' car, peering into the passenger side window, and tapping on it. My body seems to have been taken over by alien forces, or perhaps the ghost of Melody, and now my inhibitions are lowered, and even though I wonder why I have the courage to do this, I understand why it needs to be done.

The mother of the horrid girls, Carla, eases the window down and smiles at me. Her left front tooth has a smear of lipstick on it.

"Please tell your girls not to say that rhyme to me anymore," I say.

"Hmm?" She keeps smiling. "What rhyme is that, honey?"

"The one they just said. The one about fatty, fatty, two-by-four."

"I'm not familiar with that," she says. "You kids, always one step ahead of us old people."

I consider arguing with her. I consider explaining to her that this rhyme has been around since the beginning of time. In fact, I'd bet the cavemen used to say the rhyme to the largest members of the clan, but back then it was a compliment. Instead, I realize Carla is clueless, completely obtuse, and her poor daughters probably suffer from intellectual neglect.

I get my bike out of the garage and ride to school. I look down at my arms as I'm riding. I see three red bumps on my left wrist. That's all.

It is the strangest day of my life. In my first period class, which today is English, I raise my hand and answer a question about *To Kill a Mockingbird*. My teacher looks at me like she has never seen me before, and it is very likely that she hasn't. I never raise my hand in class. I hide in the back. I do not draw attention to myself. She has called me all of the following names this school year: Chandell, Chiavan, Susan, Cheyenne, and McKenzie. When I raise my hand, she doesn't even try to come up with a name, but just says, "Yes?" My answer is only one word, but I get it out without breaking into a sweat. Dr. Lawrence had said that the drug would become less disorienting over time and would leave me feeling less odd. Hazy. Disconnected.

Then it is time for accounting. If this had been any other day of the year, like a day without a yellow pill, I would have skipped accounting and avoided facing my tormentor altogether. But today is the day of the yellow pill, and someone who doesn't care has taken over my body. I walk in the door to accounting, I approach Ms. Sandell at her desk, and I say to her, "I'm on some new medication, Ms. Sandell, and I'm worried that I may need to puke. May I sit at the desk by the door and run to the bathroom if I need to?"

"Of course, Chelsea," she says. "Thanks for telling me. Just ask Tina to switch seats with you for the day. I'm sure she won't mind."

Before I turn around Ms. Sandell adds, "Oh, I have some makeup work for you."

She hands me about four pounds of worksheets and handouts, and I go sit by the door. I watch the shoes pass by me and think about the recommendations I would make to the various wearers. Lydia should not wear open-toed shoes. Her toenails have been trimmed halfway down, and the flesh puffs and swells around them. Wiley needs a new pair of tennis shoes but probably can't afford them. Lesley's heels look nice on her, but she's leaning backward way too far, pushing her knees out front to lead the way. Nicholas Dunn wears expensive-looking Nikes, and they look fabulous on him, as does everything. When he stays in front of my desk for more than a minute, I realize he's waiting for me to look up.

I realize that the medication does have limitations. I force myself to glance up, and then quickly look down again.

He smiles his greasy grin. "Thought you weren't coming back," he says. "I guess you want more than fifteen seconds of fame, huh?"

I don't reply, but he goes on.

"I can give you that," he says.

I've got my arms crossed over each other on the desktop, and I examine them. I have bumps; a few, but nothing like I've had in the past. I don't feel the rush of heat across my chest and the itchy sweatiness over my arms. While counting the bumps on my arms, I find I am able to multitask. I raise my hand, curl my fingers down except for my middle one, and flip off Nicholas Dunn.

"Ooh. Chubby Chelsea's getting feisty. I like it. I like it a lot."

Someone behind Nicholas gives him a shove and he is gone from in front of my desk. My middle finger is still in the air. I don't believe I have ever really gazed at this finger before. It's just like my toes. Long, rounded in the right places, enhanced with a strong fingernail. Even when I turn it around, I don't understand why it is behaving differently than normal. I've never flipped anyone off in my entire life. I did not know that I was capable of doing that.

Fifty

I'm walking down the hallway to lunch, but I feel like it's not me walking down the hallway to lunch. The lights are not as bright as I remember them being. No one is looking at me and usually everyone is looking at me. Even when I see Marcus Vemen, he is playing some slap-the-hands-of-your-friends game and is so engrossed in hurting members of his posse, that he doesn't even notice me as I saunter by. And I am sauntering.

My shoulders aren't curled around me, my hands aren't hidden in my armpits. I'm swinging my arms by my side, and my head is held up — I can see so much better this way. It's a weird feeling. My head is a bit fuzzy, and the truth is, I just am not wrapped up in myself. For some reason, that doesn't matter.

Melody is already seated in our usual spot in the cafeteria and when she sees me, she stands up and waves enthusiastically. Usually this would embarrass me. Today, I wave back. When I get to the table, I wrap my arms around her, squeeze hard, and then sit down. She stays standing and narrows her eyes at me.

"What is up with you?"

"What?"

"You've never given me a hug before."

"It's high time I did."

She sits beside me and gives me a hard look. "You're acting different. How come you're talking so much?"

I laugh. "I've said about ten words since I got here. That's not really that much."

"It is for you. What's up?"

I take a couple of bites of my coleslaw, chew a moment, and then speak. "I'm on medication. My head feels a bit funny, and I just don't feel as wrapped up in myself."

"Because of yesterday?"

"Yes, because of yesterday. And other . . . things."
I feel a little jittery when I say this. Am I really ready
to tell Melody what happened the night of the dance?
Will I hold together and not crumple to the floor, a used
tissue, unable to maintain form and dignity? I glance at
my arm and see no rash. I put the back of my hand to
my cheek and feel no heat. Then I say it. "And because
of Nicholas Dunn."

Melody slaps the table with her right hand and looks
at me. "What the hell did he do?" Her eyebrows are
down and her lips are straight. She's not jumping around
or talking too much or waving her hands; she's fully
focused on me and I start talking.

It feels so good to tell her. While I'm describing the
hands pushing against me, the tearing of my clothes, the
humiliation, the embarrassment, it all falls away, this
heaviness I've been carrying and didn't even notice. And
once I start, I can't stop.

I tell her about being pressed against the wall, having
my picture taken, my breasts appearing on the Internet.
It was me and my tight, risqué shirt — my risqué ways.
The assembly had been intended for me, intended to
flush me out because I am an embarrassment to the
school and have no self-respect. All of the unfairness is
right out there in the open, visible for her to see, and she

understands immediately and I want to sit close to her, feel her commiseration all the way from my fingertips to my toes. My eyes leak tears, but the release is good, cleansing, cathartic.

"That loser. That idiot. That asshole." She's worked up. "You know that what he's done is assault. He hit you. He sexually harassed and abused you. Come on. Let's go report this."

She stands and starts yanking on my arm, but I don't budge. She sits down again and puts her arm around my shoulders. "Why didn't you tell me? Are you okay? How have you been living with this?" She's on her feet again. "Let's talk to the counselor. I remember a girl in seventh grade who filed sexual harassment charges against another student and he never bothered her again. Of course she moved schools after the whole thing. I never figured out why. I'm sure it was just coincidence. Come on. If anyone can help you with this, it's the counselor."

That's when I hit the limit with my honesty, and with the pill. This drug has helped me self-advocate, has gotten me to class, has helped me look Nicholas Dunn in the eye, but it draws the line at reporting him. Why? Hmm, let me think. Maybe because then everyone will know that those were my breasts. That everyone has seen me exposed and uncovered. Obviously Nicholas Dunn shouldn't have done what he did, but now my naked self is out there and I don't want anyone putting a name to those *hooters*. I pull my arm out of Melody's grasp.

"Come on. You have to do this! Chelsea, he needs to be caught or he'll do it again. He'll think he can get away with this."

"I can't do it."

"Yes, you can. You came to school. You faced him. You can do this."

"No. Not like this. I have to do it my way."

"Okay." She nods and looks away. "You're right. I'm getting carried away. You have to do this how you're comfortable — how is that?"

"I don't know yet. But will you help me figure it out?"

Melody sits down beside me and puts her arm around my shoulders again. Her face is inches from mine and I can smell the peanut butter from her sandwich. Her blue eyes are bright and light, the pupils small, and she stares me down.

"Anything," she says. "I would do anything for you."

Fifty-one

I know exactly when the pill wears off. The bell is about to ring, and I'm sitting in film as literature II. Trevor Laats walks in the door and smiles at me. I look behind me and around me, but there is no one else he could have been smiling at. I smile back.

"Good to see you again. Were you sick before spring break?" He stands in front of my desk. His brown and blue argyle sweater vest is too beautiful for words, and his blue flip-flops match perfectly.

I open my mouth to respond, to say exactly what's on my mind, which includes something about how beautiful he is, how he's always been nice to me, how he's the kindest soul in the world and I'm pathetically in love with him, but nothing comes out. I can see myself reflected in his glasses and there they are, my Internet-sensation breasts, and I wonder if Trevor is on Facebook or Instagram or whatever the hell is being used to spread my notoriety. No matter how generous and amazing Trevor is, he will never like me because I am reprehensible and an embarrassment to the school.

"I was sick," I say and look down at his beautiful feet.

"That dance made me pretty sick too. We all should have taken that week off."

I peek up at him. He is still smiling at me, and his bow tie is still slightly off-kilter. I squeeze out a small smile and he salutes, while pivoting on his heels and taking a seat one row over.

Melody kicks me under the desk. "You never told me that Trevor Laats likes you," she says.

"Shhh," I say. "You want him to hear?"

"No, I want you to hear me. Trevor likes you. It's so obvious. You should ask him out."

"Melody, shut up, okay? He doesn't like me."

"Right," she says. She leans back in her seat and stretches her legs out, crossing them at the ankles. Today she's wearing Turkish pants, the crotch hanging somewhere by her knees, and her filmy shirt looks more like tissue paper than actual clothing. "Face it Chelsea, he likes you. And I think you might like him."

I look down at my arm. A minute ago, there had been no bumps, and now I see three patches of redness with white spots in the middle. What is wrong with me? I can handle Nicholas Dunn, but Trevor Laats gives me hives.

Fifty-two

Mom has made an appointment for me to meet with a psychiatrist who specializes in adolescent issues. When she tells me about this appointment, the medication has worn off, and I immediately develop a patch of hives across the back of my left hand. More doctors. More feelings of inadequacy.

Dr. Whitney wants to squeeze me in at the end of the week and has rearranged her schedule to do so. We, as a family, are relieved and grateful that she is making time for us. For me.

Mom explains this to me while we're eating dinner, and I am unable to swallow another bite of the Marie Callender's chicken and rice in front of me. Dad watches, and when I put down my fork, he puts his down as well. He and I make eye contact over the table. His mustache quivers and my eyes fill up with tears. Can't I just sleep through the rest of my life? Or at least through high school?

While I am working through my seven pounds of makeup work for the week when I missed school, Dad knocks on the door of my bedroom and comes in before I say anything. The bed groans when he sits, and he waits while I ignore him. Finally he starts talking, while I carefully and consciously continue to fill out conjugated "to help" verbs on a chart.

"Do you remember that psychiatrist I used to see? Three years I saw him, from seventy-two to seventy-five, and he was the reason I got into psychology in college. I've told you, right?"

He waits for me to answer, but I am trying to remember how to conjugate "they help" on the chart. I am unable to remember so I flip open my textbook in search of the right page. I am fully aware of what happened in 1972 when my dad started to see a psychiatrist and saw the same guy for three years. If he hadn't, he probably would have broken more femurs than someone with brittle bone disease.

Nineteen seventy-two was the year his brother died. Mark. He wasn't right when he came back from Vietnam. Before he'd gone, he'd really been into football like my dad, but when he came back he didn't want to do anything. He'd just lie on his bed, turn his back to everyone, and listen to Johnny Cash songs.

Dad came home from school one day, and his mom, my grandmother, met him at the door. She closed the door to the house and sat with him on the front porch.

"You can't go in right now," she'd said. "We need to wait for the ambulance."

"Who's hurt?" he'd asked.

"Mark. He's hurt very badly. Very, very badly." Dad told me that his mom started crying then, grabbing him and crying. He'd never seen her like that and it scared him. He didn't want to go into the house and see what was making his mother fall apart, but he needed to know. He tried to get away from her, go into the house, but she held on and wouldn't let him go.

"You can't help him," she kept saying, over and over. "He can't be helped."

Dad was still trying to get away from Grandma when the ambulance arrived. My grandmother has never been physically strong — she's soft and rounded, full of vanilla and powdered sugar, but Dad said that her grip that day could have choked him. She picked him up off the doorstep, even though he was almost as big as she, and she held him back while the EMT people brought a stretcher into the house.

When they came back out, Dad's brother was on that stretcher, his face covered by a sheet, and even though Dad was only thirteen, he knew what a face covered by a sheet meant. Both Dad and my grandma wailed, screamed, cried, but she never let go of him and he couldn't get away.

His brother committed suicide. Grandma had been out, picking up some groceries, and when she came back he was lying in the bathtub, his wrists slit. She'd been gone for half an hour. It turned out that he'd seen too much during his year in Vietnam and he couldn't fit what he'd seen during the war into his understanding of the world. It killed him. And then Dad met Dr. Flint. For three years he worked with him, helped him understand what had happened to his brother. Dad was so angry, so bent and unsure, that he threw himself at anyone who frustrated him, even slightly. He was a big kid, like me, and he broke so many bones that year, both in his own body and other football players', that they took him off the team. He'd changed from a gentle giant into a brute. Honestly, it's hard for me to imagine that about my dad, since he's always gentle and loving, but Grandma told me it's true.

I feel Dad's hand on my arm. I focus on what I'm writing and see the words, *ayudame, ayudame* again and again on the conjugation page. I try to blink away the fogginess of my vision, but I can't clear it. Dad's hand is a blur of hair, knuckles, and skin.

"It will be okay, Chelsea. She's going to help you."

I lay my cheek on my dad's hand, and he brushes his other hand through my hair. Under his breath, he begins to sing about miracles and wonder and promised lands. I hope it all comes true, every word, because right now I need something miraculous.

Fifty-three

The next day I wait an hour before taking the yellow pill. This way maybe it will last the entire day rather than wearing off halfway through the last period of the day.

Again, I am a different Chelsea. I'm raising my hand in class, I'm willing to work in groups, I don't hide in the bathroom when we have to role-play passive resistance in social studies. The true test comes at lunch, though, when I spot Brandy in the lunchroom. She stands in the middle of the tables, surrounded by her followers, and she's like Cleopatra, like Joan of Arc, like Ellen DeGeneres, only bigger and louder. Usually I slink under her line of sight, skulking and cowering, but I've just waved at Melody and I'm sauntering again, so she comes in for the attack.

"Just look at little Miss Curly Locks. Usually she's too good for us, won't give the WYP a second of her time, but today she's got a smile on her face, she's got a jaunty bounce in her walk, and she's on top of the world. What is up with you? Why are you Miss Happy and Sassy?"

The pill is definitely working because instead of sliding along the wall and trying to make contact with my invisible friends, I laugh out loud and think about the word sassy. Me? Sassy? No way. Never. Can't be. I like it.

"Whoa, check that out. You're even laughing today. I like this new you. You're showing the world your shit. Don't hide, honey. Don't let them make you feel bad and miserable. You're something, with your dimples and curls. You're a pretty little thing, aren't you?"

I'm standing in front of her now and I can feel the grin pushing my ears back. I again realize that I'm not all wrapped up in myself, trying to hide, trying to disappear. Why haven't I talked to this girl before? She's fantastic, she's larger than life, and she's popping happy bubbles in me like sparks and fireflies.

"I'm not little," I say.

She snorts. "Honey, what are you, five foot six? You weigh, what, a hundred seventy pounds? You're nothing, miss. And don't you dare let them tell you otherwise. You're beautiful, hon, and don't you forget that. Show your sass more often."

"How do you do that?"

"What?" Brandy says.

"Approach life so loud and bold? Have so much confidence all the time?"

Brandy tilts her head to the side and wrinkles her

nose at me. She puts her hands on her hips and she looks me up and down, from my head to my toes. It's weird, though. I don't feel judged and evaluated when she does this; I feel measured and found adequate.

"Who else is gonna stand up for you? Mommy? Daddy? No way. We're on our own in this world, and don't let that rabble out there tromp on you."

I bite my bottom lip and think about that: tromping, trampling. "What if I've already been crushed?"

Brandy leans toward me, peers into my face, and spits while she's talking. "Then you take it back."

"How?"

"Any way you can. Show 'em what you're made of. Show 'em you've got grit."

"Will you help me?"

"You know it, baby. I got your back."

Fifty-four

The idea is starting to form. Little hints of possibility appear at the corners of my mind, but I'm not used to thinking in this way — fighting back, being strong, standing up for myself — and I'm not sure I can do it. Maybe I could on the yellow pill, but I only have three of them and today is my last day.

It's weird, though; the yellow pill has made me realize how I'm supposed to act.

I feel different, like a curtain has been drawn away from a window that I could never quite look out of, and now I see clearly. I know what it feels like to walk with my shoulders back and my head held high. I realize that when I raise my hand in class and answer a question, the world doesn't end. I don't know if I can be as strong when I'm not on the pill, but I know what it feels like to be there, and I want to try. By the third day of the pill, my head isn't as woozy, and I see the world in all its shades of color.

"The integrity of the filmmaker is that she always speaks first to those she is about to film and makes sure they agree to being filmed. If they don't agree and we film anyway, we become no better than the paparazzi who film for tabloid magazines. This is your autobiography, so have respect for yourself by showing respect for others."

Mr. Butler gives us the speech every week as new people check out digital movie cameras and those who have already filmed begin the editing process. Melody and I sit at a computer in the corner of the room and edit her shots. This is my week to have the camera and I'm trying to figure out how to make my plan work by maintaining integrity as a filmmaker.

I haven't told Melody my plan. I want it to be a surprise for everyone: Melody, Mr. Butler, Nicholas Dunn, Eva McGuire, Marcus Vemen. This may be an autobiography, but I want to explain who I am and how I got here through the eyes of others.

I take the camera home and start filming that night. I ask my dad to hold the camera and focus as I paint my toes. I sing to myself while painting dark blue backgrounds and pink daisies in the foreground. Dad films with a steady hand, not asking any questions or offering any suggestions. When I'm done, I take the camera from him.

"Thanks, Dad," I say.

He nods, pulls on his beard, and looks at me.

"Chelsea," he says in his heavy bass voice.

I wait.

His eyes roam across my face, over my hair, which has been brushed and styled, and over my clothes, which are washed and clean. He looks into my eyes, and I meet his gaze. I don't smile. I don't crinkle my eyes and squeeze out my dimples. I search his face as he searches mine. The bags under his eyes never go away anymore, but bulge in black puffs. Crinkles at the edges of his eyes are a constant — not jolly crinkles, not merry crinkles, but smile crinkles. My dad isn't Santa Claus, but that's never bothered me.

"Are you happy?" he asks.

I have to blink fast. What a weird question. I bite down on my tongue to keep myself from bawling and to keep myself from talking. I think about that question, about Nicholas Dunn, Melody, *Les Misérables*, the neighbor girls, Marcus Vemen, and Trevor Laats. I look down at my chubby hands, my stomach that isn't flat, my hips that aren't narrow, and my thighs that stretch the fabric of my jeans. Then I look at my feet, which now sparkle with bright pink daisies on dark blue backgrounds. I look at my father, who bulges from his La-Z-Boy in mounds, and I think about singing with him to *Fiddler on the Roof* and *Singin' in the Rain*. I think of my mother, who is in the laundry room humming to herself and ironing her tan-and-white clothes for work.

"Are you?" I ask my dad.

We narrow our eyes at each other, furrow our eyebrows, and I watch as my dad nods a slow, careful nod.

"Yes, Chelsea, I am," he says. "I'm the luckiest man alive."

He doesn't smile as he says this; he doesn't grin and cheapen his statement. His mouth stays straight and he tugs at his beard. His brown eyes don't flicker once, the eyelids don't hide or conceal anything.

I walk to him and lay my hand on his shoulder. He places his big beefy hand on mine. I feel the warmth.

Then I take my hand away from his and walk out of the room.

Fifty-five

Dr. Whitney is exactly what I expect. Her hair is pulled tightly back into a graying bun, she wears bifocals that perch on the end of her nose, and her mouth has been pulled tight so many times, it is surrounded by creases and cracks. When I sit down across from her, she looks at me over her bifocals and folds her hands on top of the folder she has been leafing through.

"Chelsea," she says.

I wonder what she looked like when she was my age. She's rounded and soft in all the right places — her shoulders, her arms, and her waist — and she looks like she probably wears a bigger bra size than me. Were her boobs plastered on the Internet when she was my age? Of course not. When she was sixteen, electric typewriters hadn't been invented yet.

"I've been examining your file. It appears that you have been dealing with some self-esteem issues, shall we say, and have been encountering some anxiety. Does that sound correct?"

I blink.

"Let me rephrase. Why do you think you're here?"

"I fainted. At school. I break out in hives. Like now."

We both look at my arm where a bloom of red has appeared with dots here and there. I can feel another patch creeping up my neck and onto my cheek. I'm out of pills.

"Am I making you nervous?"

I hate people who state the obvious.

"Why do I make you nervous, Chelsea? Can you put your fears into words?"

I look down at my hands that are clenched in my lap. I think about how I felt when I'd taken Maxin for the last three days — I think about Brandy and how she attacks the world head-on and doesn't care what other people think. The problem is, I care. I care too much. What will this woman think of me when she finds out that my chest was exposed on the Internet? What will she think of me when she finds out that I didn't stand up for myself?

"I'm going to make a fool of myself everywhere and in all situations. Everyone is judging me."

"Is that how you feel about me?"

"What are you reading in my file?"

"Do you think that what I'm reading in your file will make me judge you negatively?"

"Well, I don't think that what you are reading in my file will make you think I should be a poster girl for self-esteem."

"Do you want to be a poster girl for self-esteem?"

Her eyebrows are up, but otherwise she hasn't moved at all, not one hair. I look at her and then I smile. I grin. She smiles back at me and we both laugh.

"I sure wouldn't want that job," she says.

"Me neither."

She might be okay. She may be the central-casting version of a psychiatrist, but after laughing with her, I realize that all those lines around her mouth are from smiling. She does it all the time.

By the end of the hour, we decide that I will continue to take the yellow pills, but every other day, not every day. I don't tell her why, but I decide this on my own, all on my own, and it is because I cannot face Nicholas Dunn without the pill, but I think I can manage on the days when he's not around.

"See you next week," she says, and I'm okay with that.

Fifty-six

The careful smile that I've perfected over the years is gone. I don't know where it went, but that false grin has disappeared. I can't muster it for the stoner in The Achievement Gap. I can't bring it to my face when I sit in Mr. Butler's class and watch *Lawrence of Arabia*. But when Trevor says hi in class, a real smile stretches across my face, and I can't reign it back in until film as literature is over.

I love meeting Melody for lunch. Having a friend in the cafeteria is like ice cream on a sunny day. It just feels right.

We're walking down the hallway toward the cafeteria while completely immersed in about half the student body, when I spot Marcus Vemen. He's bouncing around in the corridor like an unleashed puppy, and when I see him, I pull the camera bag off my shoulder and take out the digital camera, which I have until the end of the week. I hand it to Melody.

"Start filming my feet," I say to her. I say this out of the corner of my mouth. Melody drops her books in the middle of the hallway to hold the camera and starts filming.

I make my way toward Marcus Vemen, while looking past him. I don't want him to realize that I know he's there. I can tell the minute he spots me because he slams his elbow into his friend's ribs and then shoves his hands into his pants pockets. He even starts whistling.

"Marcus, do you want to be filmed for my autobiography?"

Melody follows along beside me, the camera focused on my feet, and I clutch my books to my chest while looking down. I can feel Marcus Vemen's energy; I can feel his excitement, and my body tenses in anticipation.

"Film this, sucker," Marcus says.

And then comes the hit. Marcus slams into my side, almost knocking me over, but he bounces off of me and careens across the hallway into his friends. He shakes his head, groans, and climbs to his feet. One of his friends is drinking a shake and he laughs so hard, some of it comes out his nose.

Melody is standing beside me. She is still filming, but now the camera is focused on Marcus Vemen, who is staggering around the hallway, his face scrunched tight like a pug's.

Melody puts her free hand on her hip and stares back and forth from me to Marcus Vemen.

"Shit on a brick," she says. She is wearing normal clothes today. I think I've seen her in normal clothes twice, and today she's wearing jeans and a T-shirt that says *What the . . .*

"You had better explain yourself, girl," she says to me, "because you just let that asshole walk all over you."

I pull her away from Marcus Vemen and talk in her ear.

"It's part of my autobiography," I whisper. "Trust me. I've got a plan."

"I hope so," she says. She's got her arms crossed over her chest, video camera still in one hand. Her feet are planted.

"Come on." I pull at her arm. "It's okay."

"Bullshit," she says, but she follows me into the cafeteria. She hasn't turned the video camera off, so we end up with about five minutes of Melody's T-shirt extreme close-up.

I don't really explain my plan to her. I tell her enough to pacify her, but I'm not sure how I'll put it all together yet, and I know if I tell her too much, she'll take over. I want this to be my autobiography. Not hers.

Fifty-seven

The next morning I get dressed for school, put on my yellow parka to combat the Oregon April rains, take my yellow pill that matches my parka, and stand at the front door, peering out the narrow side windows beside the door.

When the neighbor girls file out of their house in matching purple raincoats, I open the door. The video camera is in my hand and I hold it up in front of me, careful to make it obvious.

"Hey," I call over the fence between our houses. It's a low fence, painted white — a friendly fence, as my mom says. I realize as I stand with my camera in hand, my heart thumping, my hands sweating, that I have no idea what their names are. The pill has not kicked in yet. I hope I can pull this off.

I hold the video camera even higher.

"Can I film you guys in your purple raincoats?"

They line up on the walkway like purple crayons organized by size. The biggest leads the way; the youngest ends the procession. I've never looked at them this carefully before, and I see now that the middle girl, who must be about six years old, has a birthmark in the shape of a peanut on her cheek.

I turn on the camera and watch the autofocus zoom in. I hold it down, by my chest, and look through the top of the viewfinder.

"Why don't you do your song for me?" I ask, a flutter in my voice.

Without flinching, without hesitating for a moment, the three little girls open their red candy lips, show their white, evenly spaced teeth, and start the chant.

"Fatty, fatty, two-by-four. Couldn't fit through the bathroom door. So she did it on the floor. Fatty, fatty, two-by-four."

They swing their arms as they singsong, and swirl their purple coats around their legs. I notice now that the oldest girl is missing one of her front teeth and the other tooth is huge in proportion to her mouth. She looks like a lopsided beaver.

I hit pause on the video camera and look up. I smile and nod.

"That was perfect," I say.

"Are we going to be on TV?" the youngest girl asks.

"You three will be the stars of my movie," I reply.

Their mother comes out of the house and lifts a hand in my direction. I hold up the video camera, showing her what I've been doing and she smiles and nods. I nod back, turn, and head to the garage.

"Come on girls," says their mother. "The neighbor girl needs to get to school just like we do. You girls are moving as slowly as she does."

I bike to school with one hand on the handlebars and my other hand holding the video camera. I record my feet peddling. I'm wearing pink open-toed shoes that exactly match the pink of the daisies on my toenails.

Fifty-eight

When I get to school, the only person in sight is the familiar stoner, who is wedged in a corner in The Achievement Gap. He's sits on the wet ground, his head tipped back against the brick wall. I take a good look at him while his eyes are closed. He's filthy. Not obvious, covered-in-soot dirty, but grimy. The shadows under his cheekbones consist of ground-in dirt, and his hands, which rest on his knees, bear lines of black grime across their backs.

I hold my bike in one hand and cough. He slowly pulls his head away from the wall and opens his eyes like the lids are heavy. He turns his head to look at me and then attempts to focus.

I hold up the video camera.

"May I film you riding my sturdy bike?"

He doesn't seem surprised by the question. He just nods his slow nod and pushes himself off the ground. He stretches, his back arching and his spine cracking. Brown hair sticks out from underneath his stocking cap in clumps that look like accidental dreadlocks.

"Yeah," he says, "I'd like to take a spin on this beauty."

He takes the bike from me and I begin to record. He examines it, leaning it back and forth, and rubs his hand along the handlebars. He lifts the bike with two hands, one on the seat and one on the handlebars, and turns to look at me. His face has changed. Before, I'd thought he was an upperclassman, but now I realize, as his eyes are opened wide and he has a grin on his face, that he's young. Probably younger than I am. The shadowing of dirt made me believe he had stubble, beard growth, but now I see that it is only dirt.

He lifts the bike again.

"Man, it feels like a regular bike."

He swings his leg over the seat, even though it's a girl's bike, and cruises around the parking lot. He rides between the parked cars, his back straight up and down as he holds onto the raised handlebars. I should be filming him in black and white, like an old Audrey

Hepburn movie. All he needs is a girl seated in front of him.

He cruises over to me, hops off, and hands the bike back. He looks me up and down while I finish filming. His eyes are narrow, his bottom lip caught between his teeth.

"You don't really need a reinforced bike, do you?"

I give him a wink, then wheel my bike over to the rack. I lock it in place. He watches me, his hands jammed as far as they will go into his jeans pockets. His knuckles have rubbed through the pants pockets and both pant legs have holes at the knees.

"You okay with me using this footage for a class project?"

"You betcha, cap'n," he says.

I get to class late.

Fifty-nine

On Wednesday, I head to the cafeteria. I'm supposed to meet Melody there and I want her to help me. I'm not sure she will, since her reaction to the Marcus Vemen incident didn't show unconditional support.

I have a nervous lump in my throat — one I try to swallow down, but it sticks like too much peanut butter. Today is my day without the pill and I'm not sure I can do this on my own. I cough every three seconds, trying to dislodge the lump, but it doesn't work and everyone around me looks at me like I've got the bubonic plague.

Melody pats the seat next to her at our usual table near the corner, one table away from Trevor Laats. I keep my back to him so he can't watch me eat and so I don't forget what I'm doing and stare at his beautiful feet while Melody tries to hold a conversation with me.

I'm too nervous to sit. I move my weight from one foot to the other and give Melody a furrowed-eyebrow, small-grin look.

"I need your help," I say.

She looks up at me, wipes salad dressing away from her mouth with the arm of her neon pink running suit, and stands up. She wipes her hands on her thighs.

"What are we shooting today?" she asks while her eyes scan the cafeteria.

I nod toward the center of the room, the hub, the nucleus, and I can tell when she figures out what I have in mind. She looks at the ceiling and shakes her head.

"No way," she says.

"Come on, you have to help me," I say, balancing on my tiptoes. "I can't go over there by myself."

"I am not an honorary member of the WYP like you are," she says.

I open my eyes wide and bite my bottom lip. "Please?" I say.

She snorts. "All right," she says, stepping over the bench and straightening her back. "But you had better come to my rescue if she gets all up in my face."

I hand the video camera to Melody. She flips out the viewfinder and hits the power button. She follows me across the cafeteria to the WYP club.

Brandy sees us coming.

"Where's your sass today?" she thunders at me. "You're all hunkered down, got your chin tucked into your chest. I want to see that girl from before, the one with the defiance and verve."

Then she notices Melody.

"Oh yeah, this girl's got some style. I've seen her in the getups she wears, Miss Pirate one day, Miss Cleopatra the next. You got some class."

Melody opens her mouth, ready to talk back like she always does, but then she understands what Brandy just said and she stares at her, mouth open. I step in front of Melody.

"Remember when you said you'd help me?" I say. "Can I ask you some questions and film you for an assignment I have in film as lit?"

Her hands are on her hips and her face is puckered in a frown. I realize that I've never seen her smile. Never. Maybe she doesn't know how.

I motion for Brandy to come close so I can whisper in her ear. When she leans toward me, I get a hint of flowers, a taste of honeysuckle. She nods as I whisper my instructions in her ear.

"Shoot," she says, straightening her ultratight long-sleeved black T-shirt over her ultratight black leggings. She looks right at the camera, directly into the lens; Melody might as well be a tripod.

"Do you feel that you are discriminated against because of your size?" I ask her after clearing my throat. I can feel Melody's eyes watching me, but I don't look at her.

"Is that a rhetorical question?" she says.

Everything she says is loud — extremely loud. We have started to collect an audience. Students congregate around me, watching Brandy.

"Hell, yeah I'm discriminated against because of my size. Everywhere I go people stare at me, call me tubby, lard butt, jelly-belly, wide load, I've heard it all. When I go in for lunch at a fast food joint, they don't even ask if I want fries with that. They just give them to me. All anyone ever sees is how big I am. People ask me how much I weigh, like it's any of their business, and they think because I'm large, they can comment on my size like I'm a leper. Look at me." Brandy leans toward the camera, her face only about two feet from the lens. "I am beautiful. People don't see it so I tell them. Look at me. Look at my skin, creamy and smooth, no blemishes. Look at my big beautiful eyes. Those lashes are real. Look at my hands. Have you ever seen hands as beautiful as these?"

She holds them up for the camera and everyone looks. Her fingers are long, slender, like musician's hands, and the nails are painted ruby red.

"I pretend that I don't care what people think about me. You guys see me every day in the cafeteria, giving the world a hard time, but don't think for a minute that I don't feel your eyes on me, that I don't hear your comments behind my back. I see it all. I hear it all. I am beautiful. And if you can't see that, I will show you."

Brandy glares into the camera and then out toward her audience. Her eyes take in the room, daring to be contradicted. She stands, tosses her hair back, and places a hand on her hip. She looks up into the rafters of the cafeteria and shows us her profile.

She is a Viking queen.

Melody backs up, keeping the camera aimed at Brandy.

I have never before heard silence in the cafeteria. People are gathered all around us, examining the statue that is Brandy, and no one sniggers. No little freshman knocks a tray full of tomato soup into her. No asshole tries to rip open her shirt.

Then I hear a soft snap. It starts out quiet, diluted, one person softly acknowledging greatness. It feels right, like a crescendo. I look around. Trevor is standing beside a cafeteria table and snapping his fingers like you would at a poetry reading. People join him — seemingly everyone joins him. Pretty soon, the cafeteria fills with the sound of a cloud of muffled crickets. Brandy turns her head, surveys her domain, and for just a second, for a split moment that flutters away like the heartbeat of a hummingbird, I see the corners of her mouth turn up.

Sixty

I meet with Dr. Whitney again on Friday after school. She's careful with me, slow, gentle. She's not pushy like my mom but she's also not too laid-back like my dad.

She's like the porridge in *Goldilocks* that's just right.

"How were the days without the pill?" she asks.

Today I took the pill. Today was accounting with Nicholas Dunn. I'm still sitting by the door in that class, ready to run if I need to, and I've got a waste paper basket beside my desk just in case the smell of his cologne makes me puke, but even so his presence is always there, like a bad case of hives.

"They were okay. I think I get it."

"Get what?"

"How I'm supposed to act when I'm not taking the medication."

"And how are you supposed to act?"

"Well, different. Confident. I'm supposed to raise my hand and answer questions without breaking into a sweat. I'm supposed to say something when I'm working in a group instead of just sitting there and doodling on my notebook."

"Did you not do these things in the past?"

"Not since third grade. That's when I started feeling judged."

"What happened in third grade?"

"I got hooters."

Dr. Whitney waits about thirty seconds. Then she

stands up, comes around the desk, and sits in the chair beside me. She's wearing heels that are about three inches high, and I'll bet she's still shorter than I am.

"Breasts," she says. "Why would you say 'hooters'?"

"Because that's what someone called mine in third grade."

Maybe the effects of the pill are starting to wear off. At full strength, it would make me feel comfortable talking this way, but right now I want to answer in short sound bites like lightning flashes. Can you form a whole picture by looking at the world through quick bursts of truth? Probably not.

"Have you heard of the artist Peter Paul Rubens?" Dr. Whitney asks.

I shake my head.

"He made many beautiful paintings of voluptuous women. At the time when he was painting, women with wide hips and large breasts were considered desirable. I think that is still the case today. With some people."

I think about Melody flattening her shirt against her chest and showing me how flat her boobs were. I wish I were flat. Nicholas Dunn would have stayed away from me then.

"Someone took a picture of mine," I whisper.

Dr. Whitney leans closer and then reaches out to take my hand.

"Say that again, sweetheart?"

"Nicholas Dunn. He pulled my shirt down and took a picture of my breasts. Then he posted the picture on Facebook and the whole school saw. Then the principal called an all-school assembly and said that flashing your bare chest at someone showed a lack of self-respect. That was me."

A rash of red swoops up my arms, across my chest, around my neck, and onto my cheeks. I am hot and prickly everywhere; even my tears feel exceptionally warm on my lashes and dripping onto our hands. Dr. Whitney squeezes my fingers tighter and tighter as I talk.

"What is wrong with this world?" she says.

"I don't know," I whisper.

"What else did this Nicholas do?"

He called me names, he terrified me, he made me feel like Fantine in *Les Misérables*: worthless, used, and beaten. "Nothing," I say.

"What he did is not okay," she says. "You know that, right? This boy has a problem and he has pushed his problem onto you. Look at me."

I try, but it's so hard. She knows. She'll probably look up the pictures on Facebook or Instagram and see my breasts. It's all so embarrassing and humiliating. My eyes make it as far as her nose and then she puts a finger under my chin and tilts my head up so I'm looking her in the eyes.

"This is not your fault. You did nothing wrong. Your actions did not indicate a lack of self-respect. I want you to remember that when you walk through the halls of that high school."

"Okay," I say. I hear her words, I understand what she's saying, but nothing is fixed. Nothing will ever be fixed. What's done is done and no matter how many nice words this woman says, or how angry Melody gets in my defense, I still have to live with the public humiliation, and they don't. I won't ever fix this; I realize that as I sit in this comfortable room talking to this woman who seems to care. What happened will never, ever go away, but I *will* show everyone that their image of me is wrong.

Sixty-one

After needling my mom all week, she finally agrees to take me to the Calorie Counters meeting that we're no longer members of. Actually, I am still a member —

Mom paid for six months and she lets me know about it, too.

Mom sulks during the entire ride to Calorie Counters. She doesn't look at me. She keeps her hands in the ten and two positions, and she hunches over the steering wheel. I rest the camera in my lap and wonder if Bridgette will heap guilt on me too.

When I get to the clinic, Mom stays in the car, pulls out a magazine with special articles about organizing your laundry room, and then merely sniffs when I tell her I'll be back in less than an hour.

My stomach roils. Every night, even the nights when the pill has worn off, I can't sleep. My stomach grumbles and gurgles all the time and my rash flames up when I think about my project. All I'm doing is filming pieces for the video. Why am I getting an ulcer? I try to do the breathing exercises that Dr. Whitney gave me, and sometimes they work, if I can fully concentrate on the breathing and forget the demons in my life, but sometimes I can't forget and the calming breath turns into hyperventilation.

Bridgette raises her eyebrows when I walk in the door. She steps out from behind the counter and stands in front of me. She looks good as usual. She's wearing a black turtleneck sweater over a black-and-white plaid skirt. Her black tights and knee-high black boots look like they might be welded together.

"I have a favor to ask of you," I say and she waits while I explain.

When I'm finished, her only response is to purse her lips, narrow her eyes, and look at me.

"Is this your way of changing the world?" she asks.

"I thought I'd start with one classroom and work my way up." I grin at her. "Also, I'm in therapy and my doctor says I should address my fears and tackle them head-on. I'm trying to do that."

She nods slowly and then tilts her head toward the meeting room. "No video," she says. "That won't go over well here. You can record the audio."

I follow her in. The calorie-counting people sit in chairs that have been gathered into a ring. Bridgette explains that anyone who wants to talk about their traumatic experiences with being overweight may do so. Today is confession day. I hold the video camera in my lap and sit in one of the chairs. I make sure to have an empty seat on either side of me, surrounding myself with space, but my balloon cushion is short lived. Both seats are filled almost immediately. I tuck my feet under my chair and scrunch my arms against myself while practicing my breathing exercises.

"Chelsea has asked to record our meeting. She is doing a school project and feels that your comments may be helpful with the focus of her film. I have asked that she not video record, but she may make an audio of the stories. If you are uncomfortable with this, please say so." Bridgette sits and folds her hands into her lap. The other members of the circle glance at me under lowered eyelids and then purposefully ignore me. I understand their reaction; I'd do the same. Actually, I probably would have walked out.

"I would like to start the meeting with a little story of my own." Bridgette coughs into her hand. I hit the power button on the video camera, but keep the lens cap on. I don't know how to put audio over a different image, but I know it's possible. I'll figure it out.

"Most of you know that I used to weigh a hundred and twenty pounds more than I do now. When I weighed that much, I had all kinds of trouble. I didn't fit on airplanes, I found very few clothes that looked good on me, I was called names by my husband, and I didn't even like to leave the house. But when my son was two, I bought him a pass to the Oregon Museum of Science and Industry. They have a great exploratory room for children and I wanted him to experience the same things other kids experienced."

Bridgette looks around the room and then focuses on the wall somewhere over my head. I watch how many times she blinks her eyes. Twice.

"I didn't realize that to get to the toddler room, I needed to walk through a turnstile."

When she says this, I hear gasps from around the room. I suck in my breath and curl my toes into my toeless shoes.

"Yes, you can well imagine what happened. I got stuck in the turnstile. In fact, I got stuck so badly, they had to call someone from maintenance to come and take it apart. By the time I was freed, my son was having a full-blown temper tantrum and we had to leave. We never went back."

Bridgette looks down at her hands, which lie across each other in her lap. Maybe it's not true; maybe it happened to someone else. Maybe Bridgette has learned how to overcome her fears by talking about her experiences. Maybe I'm doing the same thing in my own way.

I hear a cough and refocus my attention on the next speaker. People hesitate, glance around the circle, and then begin to speak.

"I have to fly for my job. I keep telling my boss that he needs to send me first class, but he won't do it." The woman who says this is smiling. She looks very sporty in a black zip-up spandex workout suit.

"I got stuck trying to squeeze through a wooden fence on my dad's farm. I got a line of slivers on my stomach." The person who says this has long bushy hair that curls and sways around her head like Medusa snakes. Her cheeks are flushed, but the right half of her mouth is stretched out into a smile.

I whirl to move my camera from speaker to speaker even though the lens cap is on. As I work, everyone grins at me — big smiles, even.

A young girl, about my age, raises her hand. She is pretty with long blond hair that falls over her shoulders in gentle waves. She has blue eyes and thick black eye lashes. She smiles. "Just last week," she says in a quiet voice that sounds a bit hoarse, "I went to the amusement park with my physics class; we were supposed to figure out how some of the rides worked, and my assignment was bumper cars."

About ten people groan or say "no."

"Oh yeah," she says. "I got stuck in a bright red bumper car. It took me a full minute to get out. They had to stop people from getting on the ride just so I could get help extricating myself. I was so embarrassed. My entire class stared."

Everyone nods.

"Don't ever go on the Flume," a woman says who looks a bit like the former Bridgette.

"Or the Octopus," says the woman to my right.

"I couldn't get the safety bar down on the roller coaster," the pretty girl says.

"Oh shit, the Scrambler was a nightmare. I rode it with my nephew and he wanted to sit on the outside. Every time we got whipped around, I squashed him flat." The speaker of this statement, a short woman about my mother's age, laughs outright. The person next to her slaps her on the back and guffaws. I'm almost enjoying this. I can't help it. I don't quite understand what's happening here, but I'm smiling too and no one is judging me. My thoughts shift quickly, and my grin disappears. I wonder if anyone here had her breasts exposed online. I lean back in my chair. I just let the camera record the voices.

Bridgette is smiling but not laughing. When the comments die down, she speaks again, nodding her head.

"Being able to laugh at ourselves is very important. If we can't laugh, then we'll cry way too often. And it's different here. It's not like when other people laugh at us or use us as punch lines of painful jokes."

The group nods, their smiles slipping away.

"But I know the pain that you're not speaking of. I know the embarrassment, the humiliation, the criticism we feel. We live in a world designed for small people, thin people, and we don't fit."

But we should, I think to myself. We should be able to ride the rides of this world, visit the museums, enjoy the arts just like anyone else. Who the hell decided that our place is to sit at home, anonymous and lonely, while everyone else sings in unity?

Bridgette's smile is gone and her eyebrows are angled in toward her nose. The laughter has died down and I see many of the group members staring at their hands folded in their laps.

"We can do something about our inability to fit. And should. It is time for us to take control of our lives and lose some weight. Not for the world, not to ride the roller coasters, but to be healthy and to feel good about ourselves."

The group nods.

I turn off my camera, stand up, and walk out the door.

It feels like giving in; like succumbing to the pressure of the half-anorexic world around us. Why can't people like me for who I am? I do not understand and I'm not sure I ever will. Brandy would never agree to that philosophy — she'd tell these people to buck up and get sassy; stop wallowing and take on the world. I like her style, like her attitude, but her approach to the world isn't mine, nor is Bridgette's. I have to find my own way and so far, I haven't figured it out.

As I walk out the door of Calorie Counters, I weigh my feelings. I want to feel strong, to feel like I am what

I am, and I don't want to be ashamed of that. Maybe I'll never find anyone but Melody who agrees with me, but Melody is at least a start.

Well, and Brandy.

While Mom drives us home, I play back the audio and listen to the stories. I laugh out loud. That was the best Calorie Counters meeting I'd ever been to. Mom laughs too.

Calorie Counters Meeting #Not Sure

Weight Loss: Who cares?

Sixty-two

Thursday night I sleep about two hours. Every time I fall asleep, I wake up again ten minutes later in a sweat. When I get out of bed the next morning, I almost collapse. My knees shake, my head pounds, I have a twitch underneath my left eye. I stand in front of the bathroom mirror and stare at myself. I'm wearing my usual sweatshirt and jeans, and I can already feel the flush racing up my arms, across my chest, and up my neck.

Today I have to face Nicholas Dunn.

I consume my every-other-day pill while watching myself in the mirror.

I've known all week that this was coming. Today I have to get him on video. I've rehearsed what I'm going to say to him about a million times, but trying to guess his response is much easier than actually facing it.

I'm pretty sure I'll have a nervous breakdown and turn into one enormous hive right in front of him. *You can do this*, I keep saying to myself. *You can do this.*

The medication has kicked in by the time I get to accounting. I'm feeling okay, not so wrapped up in myself, but I honestly don't know how I'll tackle Nicholas Dunn. I've been telling Ms. Sandell every day that I need to sit by the door in case I have to throw up, but today I have to sit by Nicholas, and I'm not sure I will live through this.

When I arrive, Nicholas isn't in the classroom yet.

I'm so relieved that I almost start crying.

I explain to Ms. Sandell that I'm feeling much better today and would like to sit in my assigned seat.

"Have you stopped taking the medication?"

"No. I'm just getting used to it."

Ms. Sandell shakes her light brown bob, which is

perfectly straightened, without a hair out of place. She purses her lips.

"Well, fine then, but please do make up your mind." She's pretty in a polished sort of way. She always wears lots of makeup and she never smiles. "Going back and forth like this is confusing for the students around you."

I head to my original seat, the electric chair behind Nicholas Dunn that is sure to turn me into a twitching mess within the next fifteen minutes. Soon I feel a sheen of sweat building beneath my nose, behind my knees, and in the small of my back. I worry I'm going to be sick.

When Nicholas Dunn walks in, I close my eyes and will the room not to slip out from underneath my feet. Today, the day I'm not by the door, I am sure to puke all over my U of O sweatshirt.

I open my eyes. He's still standing in the doorway surveying the room. He spots me. His eyeteeth appear in his grin, his thumbs slip into his belt loops, and his eyes narrow. As he saunters over to my desk, his pelvis leading the way, my shaking finger pushes the record button on the video camera. I start recording.

I intended to ask him, very politely, if he would be willing to strut his excellent bod for the camera, but when I open my mouth, only a wheeze comes out.

"Well, look who's in her proper place," he says, his

voice silky and low. "Chubby Chelsea. Not hiding by the door anymore, huh?"

He glances down at the camera and clearly notices that it's on.

"So you want a bit of me for your permanent collection, do you? You want a bit of this?" he asks. He thrusts his pelvis at the camera, and I zoom out with my first finger so I can take in all of him rather than just his crotch. He's standing about five feet from me.

Then four.

Then three.

Other students in the class turn away — looking down at their fascinating homework, or at one another. No one notices anything. I know how it goes. Even though the room is full of people, no one sees a thing.

Nicholas's voice becomes quiet, low, full of heat and promise.

"Yo, thick chick," he says. "You came back for more, I see. You want me to flash your melons again? You need my help with that? Got a taste of fame and now you want more?" And then he leans down, whispers right into my ear, and I get a whiff of smoke. "I would offer to widen your stride, but I can see that yours is wide enough already."

I am smashed against the back of my chair. I cannot

scrunch any more in my seat. I can't breathe. My teeth are clenched together so hard that my jaw aches.

I jump up, my head making contact with Nicholas Dunn's chin. When I jump up, the desk rebels and attaches itself to my hips, falling to the floor with a heart-stopping crash. Nicholas Dunn is hit so hard in the chin that his head jerks, he steps back, loses his balance, and lands on the floor. I leap over the desk, bolt over Nicholas Dunn's legs, and head for the door. I run into the hallway, down the corridor, down the first flight of stairs I come to, and out the door. I am outside at the back of the school. The bike racks are right in front of me, and my friend the stoner is squashed into the alleyway.

I lean against the brick wall of the school and pant. I close my eyes, try to take deep breaths, and put my hand over my chest. My left hand still holds the video camera. It is still on.

After a minute, I feel the lightest of pressures, the softest of touches on my cheek. I open my eyes and look right into the dilated pupils of the stoner.

"Hey," he says. "You okay?"

My bottom lip starts to shake. I clutch my arms around me and try to convince myself that crying over Nicholas Dunn is not worth it, but my tears are unconvinced. I breathe in, deep and fast, and then it all pours out. The sound that comes out of me is loud, rhythmic, and foreign. The wail is piercing and through my tears I see the stoner back up a couple of steps. I shudder, gasp, and try to breathe.

With the back of my hand I swipe at my eyes. There is too much water, though, and all I do is spread the liquid from face to hand and back again. My hands become slick.

The stoner guy nods, continuously.

When my hiccups slow and the noise is gone, he speaks.

"That is some shit," he says. "That is some shit."

We nod together. I smear my face on the sleeve of my sweatshirt, drying some of the moisture, and then I take a deep breath. I breathe, filling my lungs again and again. The shaking slowly subsides, and when it is apparent that my heart is not going to pound its way out of my chest, I hold out my hand. It is still wet, sweaty, and salty, but I figure a bit more dirt won't hurt this guy.

"Chelsea Duvay," I say. My name puffs out in shudders. My voice is low and hoarse.

He takes my hand and shakes it.

"Matt Johnston."

I unlock my bike, get on it, and slowly pedal home. I have nothing with me but the video camera and my house keys. I don't know how or when I'll get my stuff back, maybe Melody will do it for me, but right now, I do not care. Strange, though, when I look down at my hands and arms, I see no bumps, no red rashes, no flaming skin. I spoke to Nicholas Dunn and survived.

Sixty-three

"Come on," Melody says and holds the chain up so I can crawl under it. She scampers up the stairs to the theater sound room like a squirrel up a tree, and I trudge along behind her, trying to keep her in my sight. "We only have eight minutes before we have to be back to class."

"Why eight minutes?"

"Because I told Mr. Butler we'd be back in five, so we can push the time limit to eight, but if we don't come back for ten minutes, he'll notice. Trust me. I've got this down."

I do trust Melody, on most things. Sneaking into the sound booth while we're supposed to be in class, though, is out of my comfort zone.

When we get to the sound booth, Melody pulls a key out of her ninja-costume pocket and unlocks the door.

"Where did you get a key?" I say.

"My mom. Remember? She does the costumes for the school plays."

I've never been in a sound booth before. There are way too many buttons and levers and headphones and microphones. I stand back against the door while Melody fiddles with some knobs and unplugs some wires. She points down at the theater stage, so I have to inch my way forward and look down. Something clicks in the booth and suddenly music is all around us — big, loud, full.

"You would look amazing in that fuchsia dress."

The concert choir is practicing on stage for their evening concert, which I told Melody I didn't want to attend. She has to go; she's in the regular choir, but there was no way I was sitting in the audience all by myself.

All twelve of the girls in the choir wear different colored dresses, while the boys are all in black suits with black bow ties. A boy stands at the front of the stage and he has a microphone in his hand. From the depths of his gut, from the very basis of his being, he is belting out "You Raise Me Up." Immediately the hairs on the back of my neck stand on end and I find myself leaning against the counter in front of me, my hands on the glass.

Melody turns a knob and the music in the room grows, becomes all-encompassing.

I want to sing with him. I want to be down there on that stage, matching his emotions and the beauty of the music. I want to belt out that song from the very recesses of my soul. That should be me.

Melody touches my arm and points at her wrist. Already our time is up and she touches some knobs, reattaches some wires, cuts the music off abruptly, and pulls me behind her out the door. She locks it. I look down over the balcony seats, down onto the stage where the singers look like bits of bright gift-wrapping. The sound isn't nearly as powerful here; it doesn't fill the room in waves and visible emotions, but I know what it felt like and I still tingle.

"See? That's why you have to try out. You belong up there, with them, in the concert choir."

Yes. I do. She's so right. But I'm so wrong. Those bright dresses won't fit me. Those beautiful clothes would never look good on me. I'd look like a pumpkin, like an apple, like the sun.

And when we return to film as lit, I'm no longer tingling, even though that song is still roaring through my head. I may be getting better, regaining control of myself, but I can't possibly try out for concert choir. There are some things that even renewed confidence has a hard time fixing.

Sixty-four

"The last project of the year, aside from your debut films, is a group project to be completed outside of class time. We have seen some fantastic films this semester, critiqued the character development, camera angles, editing, soundtrack, and the like. The one film we haven't been able to critique is one that I believe all film students should examine from all angles and depths. And that film is *Jaws*, directed by Steven Spielberg. Form groups of four, establish a time and place to watch the film, and have at it. You have the skills to critique films. Do it. Do it justice."

Melody kicks me under my seat and I look at her. She points a row over and I take a quick look at Trevor Laats. He has removed his glasses and is scrubbing them vigorously on his argyle sweater vest.

"Ask him to join our group," Melody mouths, but before this demand can register, and before my social anxiety can respond in the guise of hives and flaming red rashes, Trevor turns in his seat, pushes his glasses up on his nose, and looks at us.

"Whoa," he says, "*Jaws*. That is such a good movie. It's a classic. Have you seen it?"

Before I can reply, he goes on. "Do you know what a masterpiece that movie is? Did you know that real footage of a great white shark was used in the making of that film and that even though the mechanical shark looks outdated and the special effects are very seventies in nature, the film is a classic horror movie because of the absence of the shark, the actual invisibility of the demonic beast, and that absence is what makes the movie thrilling."

"Want to join our group?" I ask. The phrase comes out as one word run together, and I can tell that he has to think about what I said before he can answer. Then he gives one quick nod.

"Friday night. My house," Melody says. She hits the arm of the guy sitting one row over and one seat down. "Bill. Join our group."

Bill coughs into his hand, sits up abruptly in his seat, and grabs the edges of his desktop with both hands. He looks like his ship is about to go under and he's hanging on for dear life. "Sure," he says. "I'm in." But he doesn't look at any of us and his knuckles are so white against the desktop I'm worried he'll break something. I want to squeeze Melody, kiss her on the cheek, smash her overall-encased body in a big bear-hug, but instead I smile so big and hard, tears leak out of the corners of my eyes.

Sixty-five

For three weeks I stay after school every day to edit my film. I always choose the computer in the corner of the room, and then tilt the screen toward the wall so only I can see it. I won't let Melody help me with the editing.

"What are you planning?" she asks me, her eyes narrowed, her arms crossed over her chest. "You are not in any way going to put yourself down, are you?"

I think about that. Is that what I'm doing? Putting myself down? I don't think so. I think I'm doing the opposite. I'm showing the world — okay, just my class — how I am put down every day and what it's like to be an overweight person in this school. It's so hard to show people this, to show your classmates, people you don't necessarily trust, where your most vulnerable spot is and how that spot has developed into a body-encompassing bruise. That's how I feel, like I hurt everywhere and only a few people in my life have noticed that hurt and tried to do something about it. Yes, it's embarrassing. Yes, I want to do this. I need to do this. I think that in the end, Melody will understand.

I want my film to be a song. I want it to be rhythmic, hypnotic, revealing, and honest. I want people to feel my hurt and understand my pain, but at the same time,

I have to open myself up to them and show them that point in myself, that vulnerable spot where they could hurt me even more.

What if my plan backfires? What if, instead of showing people how much it hurts overweight people to be mocked, jeered, and tormented, they decide to use that against me and torment me even more? What if they realize that my boobs were Instagrammed around the world? It could happen.

Someone could laugh.

Everyone could laugh.

Trevor could laugh.

But I know Melody won't.

Sixty-six

"So, are you ready?" Melody asks me.

I am not ready. It feels like I have been sweating profusely all year. Today is no different. Today I am sweating, wearing my purple tunic with the gold buttons, standing in my gold and silver open-toed shoes, sporting my Irish friendship toe-ring, and adjusting my curls in the bathroom mirror.

My hands are sticky with sweat and my tongue feels glued to the roof of my mouth. There is no way I can sing.

"What are you going to sing?" Melody asks.

I search through my brain and realize that somewhere between getting up this morning, biking to school, and walking into this bathroom with Melody, every song I've ever sung has disappeared from my head. Every song has been hijacked, stolen, and twisted beyond recognition.

My heart pounds in my chest and up into my throat. I touch my neck with my fingertips, hoping the hot moisture from my hand will seep into my skin and reactivate my memories.

Nothing.

My pupils are as dilated as Matt Johnston's.

"I was thinking you should sing 'Hopelessly Devoted' from *Grease*. You know, that one you sang for me and my mom."

Melody stands beside me in the mint-green-cement bathroom at school, and we look at ourselves in the full-length mirror, which someone has tried to improve slightly by adding a border of stenciled bonnets. Whoever created the artwork is great at stenciling but not at choosing decor. And although it's quite obvious that the stencils are bonnets, someone has gone around and "changed" them into condoms by writing word *Trojan* across each one.

I gaze at the two of us in the mirror. Melody and I are opposites, like Laurel and Hardy. Today she looks like Big Bird in a bright yellow suit and matching sombrero. Neon yellow is not a good color for Melody. She looks very pale, washed out, and her blond hair looks like it's missing something next to the canary yellow of the suit. She won't tell me who she's supposed to be, and so far I'm completely stumped.

I, on the other hand, look dark next to her — olive hued. My dark brown hair with its bouncy curls and my black-lashed eyes would probably look okay in bright yellow. But putting on that suit would turn me into a lemon, whereas Melody looks more like a banana.

"Or what about a song from *The Phantom of the Opera*?"

My mouth has gone dry. All of the juices in my body are going to the wrong places. They're emerging from my pores rather than from my salivary glands. I'm pretty sure that I have contracted a fatal disease.

Melody sighs and shakes her head.

"Well, come on," she says. "Tryouts start in fifteen minutes, and I don't want to be late."

I follow Melody down the hallway and into the arts wing of the school. The only time I come down here is for mandatory assemblies like the holiday concert or diversity day. I've never been in the band room. I've never been in the choir room. I was in the theater for the first time when Melody and I broke into the sound booth. As I traverse the hallway behind Melody I try to understand why the floor feels like it is buckling and why the walls feel like they are closing in. I have taken my medication. Why is it not working? I am going to stand in front of someone I've only seen from a distance and try to sing in front of her. What was I thinking when I agreed to do this?

Okay, so sometimes it is very difficult to say no to Melody. She says all the right things, like how I sing like an angel and how my voice should never be relegated to the shower. She didn't, of course, say a thing about how no one in the choir will want to stand anywhere near me because I'm overweight and don't have any friends. She forgot to mention that. Oh that's right, she's my friend. She might take it personally if I mention that no one likes me.

It's eight o'clock. School hasn't even started yet, and already there are ten people sitting in chairs or pacing back and forth in front of the choir room. Almost all of them are singing to themselves in smooth vibratos and high-pitched keens. A voice singing scales comes from behind the bathroom door across the hall. Melody high-fives with a very poised guy with carefully shellacked hair. He doesn't stop singing. He nods to us, and we walk near the door to the choir room.

My name is eighth on the list. Five names before mine have already been checked off. I clutch my hands in front of me. I grab my arms and hug myself. I try to think of a song, but nothing pops into my head.

Melody pulls on my arm and then sits beside me in one of the chairs. She hums. She's been in the regular choir for two years already even though she claims she can't sing. She can sing. She just doesn't have a big voice, not like her personality.

The choir door suddenly opens and a student emerges. The girl is tiny, birdlike, with petite features that look a bit pinched. She has tears in her eyes and is sniffling. A friend throws her arm around her shoulders and the girl sobs loudly. "My voice cracked on the high C."

She wails and I shiver. A student aide follows the girl out the door and checks a name off the list. Then he looks down at his clipboard and announces the next name.

"William Weber."

The guy who gave Melody the high-five straightens his buttoned-up shirt, adjusts his tie, and runs a hand over his hair.

"Hahahahaheeheeheeheehohohohohuhuhu . . . ," he chants as he enters the room.

The door closes behind him.

I swipe my hands on my pants, jump up, and pace the hallway. I try to sing to myself, hum under my breath, but nothing comes out.

Melody is next. When she disappears into the room, she flashes a grin at me and tips her sombrero in my direction. Then she turns, slides into the room, and the door shuts me out.

I sit in a metal chair and grab onto my seat like I'm on a roller coaster. I have lines from songs flitting through my head, but nothing whole, nothing I can hang on to and cling to. I take a deep breath and then look down at my shirt, worried that I popped a gold button. I jump up and run to the bathroom, having to go pee for the seventieth time in ten minutes.

The shirt looks fine. In fact, when I glance at myself in the bathroom mirror, I look amazingly normal. I should be green by now or maybe even rainbow striped, considering the emotions turning my stomach. I should look like a kaleidoscope with triangles, prisms, stars, and hearts turning circles on my face. Instead it's just me.

When I emerge from the bathroom, Melody is coming out of the choir room followed by the student aide. She grins at me, shrugs her shoulders, and says, "Nothing to it."

The student aide calls out loudly, "Chelsea Duvay."

Melody gives me a quick hug, turns me around, puts her hands on my shoulders, and marches me toward the choir room door. I creep through and it shuts. I glance back quickly and Melody is already gone. I take two steps forward. The room is huge, octagonal in shape, and lined with bleachers. In the middle of the room sits a grand piano, and beside the piano sits Mrs. Bryant-O'Shea in a high-backed swivel chair. She wears a light-gray suit and black pumps. She looks at me over the top of her glasses before she reads from the clipboard in her hand.

"Chelsea Duvay. Currently a sophomore. Have you gone to this school for the last two years?"

Everything she says sounds polished — carefully annunciated. All her T's sound crossed, all her I's sound dotted. I wonder if she ever uses contractions.

I clear my throat.

"Yes," I say. I have to say it again, though, because I'm not sure I said it out loud the first time.

"And why have you waited until your junior year to try out for concert choir?" When she says this, her eyes go up and down my body, tucking and adjusting.

I blink, feel the weight of her eyes evaluating, the unspoken judgment settling around me like broken glass, and I feel the nervousness ooze out of me. In its place, the anger begins to build — bricks and bricks of deep red anger. I stick out my chin. I narrow my eyes, and then I throw my shoulders back and take a deep breath. Heat surges through me, starting from my open-toed shoes and flowing up into my cheeks. Her eyes flow over me one more time and then she makes a slight motion with her hand, a shooing away of a gnat, and I begin.

As soon as I open my mouth and the words come out, I know I've chosen the right song. I don't actually remember choosing the song, but here it is, flowing from my mouth in waves. I don't know if it will get me into the concert choir or not, but all my anxiety, all my nervousness, my stacks of anger, come belting out from *Les Misérables*. I start out low and full, just like the song does, breathing through those heavy notes, and then I rise in pitch and in volume. I close my eyes and fill the room with voice.

"Do you hear the people sing

Singing a song of angry men?

It is the music of a people

Who will not be slaves again."

And when the last notes float out of me and wing

their way around the room, I open my eyes.

Mrs. Bryant-O'Shea is holding her reading glasses in one hand. Her pen is poised in her other hand, about two inches above the clipboard. Her mouth is open just slightly and I can see the tips of her front teeth peeking from beneath her bright red lips.

"Good God, my girl," she says. "Where did you come from?"

And then I slide backward, shuffling my feet to keep myself from falling, and when the back of my legs hit the riser, I land heavily on the bottom step. The room spins around me, twirls, pulses, and then it rights itself. I rub my hands up and down my arms. The rash is light red, not flaming, and I see only three hives. I flex my ankles, stick out my feet, examine the purple tulips on my toenails and the ever-faithful friendship toe-ring.

I'm okay.

Sixty-seven

Melody makes me come over half an hour before Trevor Laats and Bill something-or-other for our group project, and we get the snacks ready. Dad made a double batch of his macadamia nut caramel popcorn and a batch of his caramel brownies to celebrate the momentous occasion of my first almost date. Even Mom got into it and helped Dad in the kitchen by getting the ingredients out of the cupboard while Dad shouted out what he needed.

"Baking soda!"

"Check."

"Unbleached flour!"

"Check."

"Sea salt from the Dead Sea."

"Not sure we have that, honey. Is this iodized salt okay? What does *iodized* mean?"

"Just give me the salt."

"Check."

Mom didn't even tell me how many Calorie Count points were in half a cup of the macadamia nut caramel popcorn, and trust me, I didn't ask.

Melody is more excited than I am. She rushes me into the TV viewing area and shows me where everyone is supposed to sit — me and Trevor on one side of the L-shaped couch and she and Bill on the other side. Then she rushes me back into the kitchen where she pulls three different types of soda from the fridge, and then almost starts crying because she's just sure that the won't like Dr Pepper and why did she choose Dr Pepper instead of just plain Coke, and honestly, no one likes Mountain Dew anymore, what was she thinking.

"Melody," I say.

"And Mom made me get blue chips instead of Doritos because she says Doritos have MSG in them, but no one likes blue chips and everyone loves Doritos so I don't know —"

"Melody," I say again, and I put my hands on her shoulders. I squeeze hard, trying to hold her in place while she prances up and down and looks everywhere but at me. "It's a school project. That's it, that's all."

"But I want them to like me. I want them to like my house."

"I get that. But you know what? I like you. I like your house. That's what matters, right?"

Melody stops bouncing up and down and finally slows down enough to look at me. She puts her hands on my shoulders like we're doing some weird wrestling move, and she gives me a careful smile.

"Okay."

The doorbell rings, but instead of Melody racing across the room and throwing the door open, she carefully lowers her arms, I carefully lower mine, and together we walk to the door. On the count of three

Melody opens it. Trevor stands right on the top step, but Bill shifts his feet back and forth on the bottom step and his hands hang taut at his sides, drumming quiet but frantic beats into the sides of his legs.

With a calm, open-armed flourish, Melody sweeps her arm into the room and says, "Welcome."

Trevor heads right for the TV and picks up the DVD case of *Jaws*. He flips it and reads the back.

"Oh, you're right, Bill. It is Lorraine Gary who plays the police chief's wife. I kept thinking it was Sally Kellerman, but that wouldn't make sense. Not really," Trevor says, like the truest movie geek you've ever heard.

He sits down on the wrong side of the sectional couch, and I can see Melody grabbing at her skirt and hopping up and down when he does. Bill hasn't even entered the room yet, and is still standing in the doorway. I think for a minute that he's going to turn around and make a run for it, so I pick up the extra-credit assignment sheets and bring one over to him before he can bolt.

"I'm pretty sure we each have to fill out our own," I say as I hand him the form.

He nods solemnly and lifts his right hand to take the paper while his left hand continues its frantic musical movement.

"You play guitar?" I ask.

"Keyboard," he says.

"I sing."

"Like what? Adele? Lady Gaga? Miley Cyrus?"

"Um, I like musicals."

He curls his left hand into a fist and holds it out in front of him. I fist bump, move to the side, and shut the door to the house when he takes a step forward. He's in. We're all in. But I don't know what happened to Melody.

"I'll be right back," I say and walk calmly down the hallway to Melody's bedroom. She is curled up in the corner of her room with her arms over her head and her butterfly wings squashed against the wall.

"This was such a mistake. This was such a mistake," she mutters over and over again.

I march across the room, pull Melody's arms away from her head and squat in front of her.

"Stop it."

"What?" she says, looking up at me. Sweat sparkles on her face.

"You have guests. Those boys are sitting in the other room as scared as you are, and you're in here hiding. Pull yourself together. This is your house, your safe place, and you're making them feel uncomfortable."

"But he sat in the wrong spot."

"So we'll get him to move."

"How?"

"Watch me."

I march back out of the room and down the hallway. Both boys are sitting together filling in some information on the assignment sheets while checking the movie cover. I cough lightly into my hand and they both look up. Until this moment, I'd been fine. No rashes, no hives, no wobbling voice, but when I know that I need to address Trevor and fix the seating issue, I'm suddenly self-conscious and feel the heat rising across my chest. *Chelsea, you can do this.*

"Trevor, will you help me in the kitchen a minute with the snacks?"

"Sure," he says and jumps right up. As soon as the spot beside Bill is vacated, Melody saunters across the room and sits down next to Bill. He glances at her quickly and then looks away. She pulls her feet up on the couch and examines the sparkling blue fingernail polish on her toes.

"I, uh, like your wings," Bill says.

"You do? I mean, do you? My mom made them. My mom makes all of my outfits, you know. She made . . ."

Trevor and I walk into the kitchen area of the open

room. I point to the trays on the counter that have three different selections of soda, a bowl of blue chips, macadamia nut caramel popcorn, caramel brownies, and carrot sticks. Trevor points to the carrot sticks.

"Melody's mom make you include these?"

"Yeah," I say and laugh.

And Trevor laughs with me.

"My mom would do that too. I think all moms are preprogrammed to embarrass their kids."

"You get along with your mom?" I ask.

"Sometimes. She hates the way I dress," Trevor says.

"I love the way you dress."

I gasp but try to cover it. I'd taken the social anxiety pill just for this occasion, just so I could function in a room full of social-ness, and once again it is working too well. I'm able to say things and deal with situations that would have left me cowering under the table before. Trevor takes off his glasses and cleans them on his argyle sweater. He looks up at me, his glasses still in hand, and I get a good look at those amber eyes with gold highlights. They're more beautiful than his feet.

"I've been meaning to tell you how much I like your shoes," Trevor says. "Your feet are just perfect. I mean, really. I've never seen feet like yours." He pops his glasses back on his face and picks up the tray from the kitchen counter. His hands tremble. When I pick up the other tray, mine do too.

Sixty-eight

I hate going to the mall. Going to the mall always makes everything I am in life, and everything I am not, all too clear.

Most stores do not cater to the plus-size crowd. Most stores cater to the I'm-super-skinny crowd. I never understand why they organize the stores the way they do. I walk through the main doors of the mall and immediately pass one of those skinny stores where every model in the display window, every skirt, skort, shirt, blouse, tunic, top, tee, capris, bra, negligee, sock, and stocking for that matter is displayed in size negative ten. Every article of clothing in the store window is displayed for someone else. Someone other than me. I try not to acknowledge those stores.

But then, right next to the store for the dangerously thin, there is a Cinnabon. I gain weight just walking past that store since the smell is so rich and caloric it settles around my hips like pure lard. This store is intended for me, and when I walk past the counter, I can feel the eyes of the workers following me down the corridor, waiting for me to turn and demand half a dozen cinnamon rolls. Just past Cinnabon is another skinny-girl-only store. Whoever was in charge of organizing the retailers must have been smoking pot that day. There is no other explanation for the layout. What they should do is stick the heavy-calorie stores near the plus-size stores. That, at least, would make sense, even if the hinting wouldn't be very subtle.

The only reason I am in the mall is because I want to buy *The Goodbye Girl*, the musical, for my dad. Jackie recently made all the costumes for a production of the musical, and Melody has been singing the songs to me all week at school. The songs are awesome. I know my dad will like them. But I don't want to buy the DVD off the Internet because I'd have to use Dad's credit card, and then it wouldn't be much of a surprise.

I walk past about ten clothing stores, two trinket shops, three smoothie places, and four food counters selling good-smelling items that I refuse to consider, and then I find myself in the middle of the mall. There's a special display today, and it doesn't involve food of any kind.

The Humane Society has taken over the central court and they have rows and rows of animal cages circling the open area. People are ambling past, peering at the puppies, pointing at the dogs, stooping down to pet something in a large metal tub.

I make my way around the cages. The puppies are cute, but have way too much energy. They remind me a bit of Melody, all that jumping, panting, and demanding. The grown-up dogs are more mellow, but most of them seem to be of the slobbering species. They range in size from miniature pug-ish to huge Great Dane-ish. I observe, but pass by.

The metal tub is fast approaching with a crowd of people around it ooh-ing and aah-ing. I peer over a couple of shoulders into the metal basin and see six Siamese kittens mewing, batting, and rolling over one another. I try to squeeze my way between a couple of seven-year-olds to get a closer look at the kittens, but so many hands are reaching toward them, so many fingers are stretching and touching, that I feel overwhelmed and squeeze my way out again. I continue along the row of cages.

This row is much quieter. The cages are filled with adult cats. I watch as a Humane Society worker in a bright orange vest opens a cage for an elderly woman. The elderly woman slowly lays her cane at her feet and then eases back up into a standing position. With both hands she reaches for a plush gray cat. She drapes the cat over her shoulder and lays her head against its side. Then she turns, shuffles to a bench a few feet away, and rubs a bony white hand across the thick coat. The cat closes its eyes and rests its chin on the lady's shoulder.

I keep moving, gazing into the cages. Most of the cats are solid black in color, or a mix of white and black. One of them is calico and another is a brownish-black mix with long fur. They all peer at me dolefully, or curl their heads away from the people into their paws and their loneliness. As I continue to walk, a bizarre yodeling sound rises in pitch. It's a strange sound, a deep-in-the-throat cry that makes the hairs on my arms stand up. I peer into the cages, but can't quite figure out where the sound is coming from. I look around, but no one seems to be paying any attention. And then I see a worker in an orange vest holding a calico cat. The worker is scratching the cat under the chin and the cat is yowling, gurgling, shrieking. I smile.

The worker looks up. She is a middle-aged woman with brown eyes and an open smile. I walk up to her and watch as the cat continues to make its noise.

"She's a singer, this one," the woman says. "Whenever she gets loved, she starts to sing. Rub her here."

I reach out my hand and rub the cat around the ears. It opens its mouth as if to yawn, and out comes a hum. It's not a terrible sound, just surprising, and I grin at the woman.

"Want to hold her?" she asks.

I nod.

The woman hands the cat to me and I feel the weight of fur, warmth, and muscle in my hands. Cats are so smooth, so flexible and bendable. When I hold the cat, she molds into me and hums her soft vibrating purr. I sit down on the bench and snuggle her against my chest. I rub my chin in her fur and hum along. The two of us vibrate together, purr our songs, and I push my nose into her softness. She smells of comfort and heat. I hug her against me.

The worker is standing beside me with a small smile on her lips. She waits for me to hand the cat back so she can slip the feline into the cage and shut the door. But I can't do that. I can't imagine pushing this beautiful creature back behind a door and locking her away where her songs won't be heard.

"How much is she?" I ask.

"You pay for her shots, that's all," says the worker. "Thirty dollars."

I reach into my pocket, pull out the money I'd meant to spend on my dad's DVD, and I purchase the cat. I don't even know how old she is, what her story is, what her name is, but I don't care. This cat belongs with me.

I am given a small cardboard carry case to take the cat home in. I board the bus, hugging the carry case to my chest and humming softly to the cat. Her name is

Isabel and she is probably about six years old. She was brought in to the Humane Society about two months ago — no tags, no name, no history. No one has come to ask about her.

I've never had a pet. I've never owned a cat. My mom can't stand animals in the house, how they shed and leave fur bunnies underneath the couches. Mom is going to kill me, and even though I know this and even though I understand that now I'll have to use my dad's credit card to buy the DVD for him, I smile all the way home and sing happy songs deep in my throat.

Sixty-nine

I will never be a movie producer.

My film runs four and a half minutes long, but I spent thirty hours editing it. How does anyone make a movie that lasts two hours? It would take me a lifetime to make a movie that long. I'll stick to my plan to open my shoe store or become a world-famous singer, and I'll leave the art of editing to those who have the patience for it.

Like Trevor Laats. His movie lasts fifteen minutes. Trevor works with autistic children on a horse ranch. Every weekend he goes to this horse ranch and helps kids who can't talk, kids who can't stand human touch, kids who are so wrapped up in their own worlds, they don't see the one around them, by leading them on horses. He teaches the kids how to groom the animals, how to hold the reigns, how to touch and care for the horses, and sometimes even how to ride the horses at a gallop. His video consists of his introducing some of the autistic children and showing them gain confidence and happiness by riding horses.

I watch Trevor carefully, although surreptitiously. I keep my head faced toward the movie he has made while watching his movements out of the corner of my eye. He is leaning forward in his desk, his arms squashed between the desk and his body, a small smile inching up the corners of his mouth. His beautiful feet, in their sandals, are crossed over each other at the ankle underneath his seat. He spiffed up his outfit today by wearing a light blue bow tie that matches his argyle sweater vest.

His movie is good.

He doesn't focus on himself the whole time like many people in the class have done. He shows us who he is in conjunction with the autistic kids he works with, and in that relationship, I see a whole different person. I see someone who isn't quiet, who isn't shy or reserved. This Trevor Laats in the movie throws back his head and laughs out loud when the kids smile or say something silly. This Trevor Laats doesn't wear glasses, but displays patience and calm even when the kids make strange sounds or scream.

Sometimes when you get to know someone better, you don't like them as much. Like my Grandpa Reece. In Trevor's case, it is the opposite. I know him better now and I like him even more.

Melody shows her film, which is hilarious. Thirty times we see her emerge from her house in a different outfit, but each time the shot only lasts a couple of seconds so thirty times becomes about two minutes — two minutes of Melody wearing wild clothes. Her film is fast, hyper, and intense. It is over in five minutes and we all have to relax, sit back in our chairs, and take a deep breath. If she ever does a full-length feature film, her audience members will all have heart attacks.

We are going in the same order as we checked out the camera. My film is last, after Marcus Vemen's. Marcus has made a ten-minute film that involves him laughing with his friends, skateboarding, laughing with his friends again, and doing illegal things like spray-painting the side of a building and smoking. I have learned nothing new about Marcus Vemen and I do not like him any better.

Last night I slept like a baby. I shouldn't have, considering that today I am about to reveal my soul to the class. I am about to put my humiliation on display and hope no one laughs. But last night I had my true film debut.

I showed it to my family.

My grandparents came over just for the occasion. They brought three different kinds of popcorn. I told them that the film was four and a half minutes long — we wouldn't even have time for popcorn, but they insisted on bringing it anyway. The five of us, Grandma, Grandpa, Mom, Dad, and I, sat in the living room and watched the film. It went something like this:

A shot of my feet while I am humming.

The neighbor girls chanting, "Fatty, fatty, two-by-four."

Another shot of my feet walking down the hallway at school when suddenly . . .

I am smashed into by Marcus Vemen. He and his buddies practically have heart attacks they're laughing so hard.

Then I go back to the neighbor girls chanting, "Couldn't fit through the bathroom door."

Then my dad's shot of me painting daisies onto my toenails while I am singing a song from *Les Mis.*

Next is a shot of Matthew Johnston asking me about my very sturdy bike.

I return to the neighbor girls chanting, "So she did it on the floor. Fatty, fatty, two-by-four."

And then I have the hardest segment. I show Nicholas Dunn. I have edited it so he says parts of his speech three times in a row: "Yo, thick chick," he says. "You come back for more? You come back for more? You come back for more? I would offer to widen your stride, but I can see that yours is wide enough already. Wide enough already. Wide enough already."

Then there is another shot of my feet, but no humming this time. The polish on my toenails is chipped and worn.

I go back to Matt Johnston where he says, "You don't really need a reinforced bike, do you?"

I filmed the next segment of the film without my family knowing. We'd been watching *Fiddler on the Roof*, and when the song "Sunrise, Sunset" came on, the room had filled with song when we all sang along.

The Calorie Counters segment comes next, with the overweight people telling their stories, laughing about them, and I overlay their comments with a shot of Matt Johnston riding my bike around the parking lot of the school.

Brandy comes next: "I pretend that I don't care what

people think about me. You guys see me every day in the cafeteria, giving the world a hard time, but don't think for a minute that I don't feel your eyes on me, that I don't hear your comments behind my back. I see it all. I hear it all. I am beautiful. And if you can't see that, then I will show you."

And then the last image is of my face, belting out the song from *Les Misérables* that I sang for choir tryouts.

When the film ends, my family is quiet. I stare down at my feet, waiting for some sort of reaction. I hold the remote in my hand and click "stop" about fifty times. I know it's not a great film; I don't have the angles right all the time, usually I don't even consider the lighting, but I think it gives the world a pretty good image of who I am in contrast to how I am perceived.

My grandma is the first to react. She is sitting next to me on the couch and puts her arm around my shoulders. She leans her head against mine and we sit together for a few minutes. Mom blows her nose in a tissue. Grandpa is the one who speaks.

"I remember all that," he says. "Kids haven't changed a bit."

"The neighbor kid, Richard Benson, used to squeal like a pig whenever he saw me," says my dad.

"Didn't you beat that boy up after football practice one time?" Grandma says.

Mom blows her nose again. Isabel rubs up against her pant leg and leaves a trail of fur in her wake.

"You should earn best picture for this one, honey," Grandpa says. "You've captured the plight just right."

After that we watch *Oliver Twist* and eat every bit of the popcorn.

And so I sleep like the dead, calm and happy. Isabel purrs against me, rumbling warmth into me, and I don't care at all about Marcus Vemen, Eva McGuire, or Nicholas Dunn.

Seventy

And even in class, when my film begins, I'm not really that nervous. My heart thumps in my chest a couple of times and I clutch my hands together in my lap, but my cheeks aren't flushed, I'm not sweating, and the room isn't spinning around me. Melody jumps up from her seat when the movie begins and throws an arm around my shoulders, giving me a quick squeeze, and then she sits down again. I'm able to smile at her. She smiles back.

When the scene with Marcus Vemen plays, he turns a strange shade of purple from the corners of his mouth up into his hairline. When images of my painted toes come on the screen, I see Trevor glance at my feet. As the nasty comments are played again and again, I feel Melody's hand on my back. And then I see Eva McGuire drop her mouth open when Nicholas Dunn says three times that he'll widen my stride.

When the film is over, I'm not sweaty. I'm not covered in hives. I'm not crying. This is my life. And it has shaped who I am. *This is the music of a people who will not be slaves again*, and everyone in the world should understand that.

As Mr. Butler hits stop on the remote, it is quiet in the room. No one laughs, but it takes a few seconds before anyone claps.

And that's okay.

I look at Mr. Butler and he is watching me. Carefully.

"Time for a break," he says and claps his hands. Then he wiggles his finger at me. I look at the distance from my desk to his and I wonder if I'll actually be able to make it. The twenty feet elongate and stretch and I worry that the floor will bubble under my feet or open up a black hole and suck me in.

Somehow I make it over to Mr. Butler's desk. He points at the chair beside his desk and I sit in it. I glance up at Melody across the room and she is watching me, both of her hands clasped together on her desktop.

"Chelsea Duvay. That was a stunning piece of work. Perhaps the editing is a bit rough, but the statement made through the images is powerful and profound. I would give your film five stars."

A smile wobbles onto my face, but doesn't last long. I can feel more coming and I'm not sure I want to hear it.

"Sometimes films create discomfort in the viewers, something that leaves us thinking about our actions and our thoughts. You've done that here, Chelsea, and I think everyone in this room will be thinking about your autobiography for a long time to come. Me included."

Mr. Butler holds out his hand, and I shake it with my sweaty, hive-free palm. He doesn't smile at me and I don't smile at him. And that's okay. He's seen me for who I am, what my life is like, and even though my film didn't get a standing ovation, it was honest and true.

Seventy-one

After school we walk down the street to the coffee

shop. Melody impulsively asks Bill and Trevor if they want to come with us and both of them say yes even though I know that means Trevor will miss the bus.

Ever since the movie at Melody's house, he's been talking to me. And I've been talking back. We say little things like, "I can't wait for summer vacation," and "Star Wars and Disney just do not mix."

At the coffee shop I sit in a booth across from Melody and try not to move. Somehow the seating worked out perfectly and Trevor is sitting beside me and Bill is sitting beside Melody. All of us are laughing because Melody is explaining why she doesn't do gymnastics anymore even though she did it for years as a kid, and this has something to do with Melody's inability to control her arms and legs, which she is waving around spastically while standing on the bench seat. Bill is laughing so hard, he has put down his spoon and is holding his napkin to his eyes to keep them from leaking into his ice cream. Trevor chuckles now and then, and I muster a smile, but really neither of us is paying much attention to Melody because Trevor's hand is on the bench between us, and my hand is on the bench between us, and somehow, strangely, our hands have inched closer together and now his pinky finger is touching mine, and I can't move, I can't breathe, and I can't believe this is happening.

Melody does not seem to care that we are barely

paying attention to her, and I realize in this moment that I am not just enduring, existing, and holding on. I'm happy. I like these people. Oddly enough, they seem to like me too. And in this moment, I don't care about Nicholas Dunn or the fact that he revealed my breasts online to thousands of viewers; in fact, I was a different person then and that was a different time.

I still have beautiful feet, and I'm still overweight, but I've noticed that others see me for who I truly am. Somehow, through all the crap of this semester, not only did I make friends, and not only do they like me, but I was able to step outside and past my deficiencies and show the world my true self. This is me. All of me. And that may involve being overweight, but I'm more than a number on a scale and a BMI measurement. I'm more than a sum of my parts. I'm Chelsea Duvay: I sing, I love musicals, I'm going to open my own shoe store, I have friends, and I have beautiful feet. And that's what truly matters.

Acknowledgements

Thank you to my teen beta readers, Makaena Durias, Kat Lindsey, Rachel Ohm, and Corban Woosley, and to my writing group readers, Laura Byrd, Kelly Garrett, Robin Herrera, Miriam Forster, and Kristina Martin. The positive criticism, help, and unwavering enthusiasm from my agent, Dawn Frederick, and my editor, Nick Healy, kept me grounded and encouraged. Thanks, always, to my family for their positive, patient support.